So Who's
Arguin'

Buck Halliday fled the town of Pardoo after being falsely accused of murder. In his haste to avoid a lynching, he strayed from the main trail and ended up in a desolate valley with a bad reputation. They said plenty of men had ridden into the nameless valley, but none had ever returned.

It wasn't long before Halliday discovered why.

Almost before he knew it, he was fighting for his life against a vicious clan led by a madman named Masterson, and his only hope of salvation lay with the very posse that was trailing him, and determined to make sure he kept his date with the noose!

So Who's Arguin'

Adam Brady

A Black Horse Western

ROBERT HALE

First published by Cleveland Publishing Co. Pty Ltd,
New South Wales, Australia
First published in 1967
© 2020 Mike Stotter and David Whitehead

This edition © The Crowood Press, 2020

ISBN 978-0-7198-3130-0

The Crowood Press
The Stable Block
Crowood Lane
Ramsbury
Marlborough
Wiltshire SN8 2HR

www.bhwesterns.com

Robert Hale is an imprint
of The Crowood Press

Typeset by
Simon and Sons ITES Services Pvt Ltd
Printed and bound in Great Britain by
4Bind Ltd, Stevenage, SG1 2XT

ONE

A NOOSE FOR A NOTCH

Buck Halliday stood with his feet planted wide, his hands tied behind his back and a gag stuck in his mouth. Swinging slowly back and forth before his eyes was a length of rope with a noose tied at the end, and under the play of the hot wind, the knot kept hitting him on the forehead.

It was fair to say he'd known better days.

If Halliday preferred to be somewhere else, nobody in the crowd of thirteen men and one woman had the slightest notion. They had been starved of excitement for so long a hanging would make their day. Even Lizzie, who only yesterday had professed a yearning desire to lay naked beside Halliday's muscular body, today seemed

5

to be enjoying his discomfort. He tried to catch her eye, hoping to get her to speak up for him. But Lizzie seemed more interested in tugging at the yellow ribbon which barely held her blouse together across her full young breasts. She had the complete attention of eleven of the thirteen men present. The exceptions, as Halliday saw it, were her father, Nathan Coglan, and her younger brother, Joel.

A towering, skeletal figure in black broadcloth coat and grubby Levi's, Nathan was holding a battered Bible toward the heavens, eyes closed, face stern, lips barely moving, while his son was idly tossing his six-gun from one hand to the other.

There was not a sound on the hilltop, apart from a slight rustle of leaves as the hot wind blew through the upper branches of the hanging tree.

Halliday willingly endured the silence and inactivity, happy to have his stay on this earth prolonged as much as possible. It had been a charmed life, perhaps not the kind to earn the congratulations of money-hungry and ambitious men, or have the unconditional approval of hardened lawmen, but it had its moments and its memories. Now he simply wanted to make it last a little longer ...

While Nathan prayed silently to the heavens and Joel continued to fool with his gun while the others lecherously eyed Lizzie's ribbon — or what delicates lay beneath it — Halliday pondered the fickleness of fate that had brought him here.

There was no denying that he was guilty — guilty of killing a mean-tempered, sour-bellied cowhand who had tried to carve up his face with the jagged edges of that broken bottle.

What was behind Dace Mooney's attack?

The answer, Halliday told himself, just as he had told this lot looking up at him a dozen times over, was Mooney simply didn't want him around. Halliday had bested him, though the outcome had been close, in a shooting contest held to celebrate Pardoo County's twentieth year of existence. The prize was fifty dollars, but as an added incentive, Lizzie had offered her services to the winner — free of charge, of course.

She had come to Halliday's room above the saloon and stripped naked in eager anticipation of honoring her part of the prize. It had taken Halliday some time to convince her that he didn't want to overstep the limits of the town's hospitality — especially when her father, brother and Dace Mooney believed she was soon to become Dace's wife.

Each man had individually warned Halliday to keep well away from her.

Halliday wondered if his refusal to claim the prize had anything to do with her seeming disinterest now in whether or not his neck was stretched. He was never sure about the thinking processes of women, especially women like Lizzie. Without laying a hand on her gorgeous, naked and willing body, which he knew he would later regret, he'd gone downstairs for a drink.

Mooney caught sight of Lizzie leaving Halliday's room and came to the obvious conclusion. He'd broken a bottle and charged, but Halliday had knocked him to the floor with a straight right flush to the jaw, then stomped down hard on his wrist.

Joel then decided to buy in to the scuffle, and Halliday had dispensed with him, too. Then, before Halliday had time to explain, Mooney had drawn his gun and had started using him for some well-needed target practice.

Halliday hit the floor, saw young Joel go down again, struck by one of Mooney's stray bullets, and had done what a hard life and plenty of tight corners had trained him to do.

He'd shot Dace Mooney and killed him.

Because the Coglans were a long-established family in Pardoo County, and it was generally believed that young Lizzie's innocence had been defiled, the sheriff had washed his hands of the whole affair. Accordingly, Nathan ordered Halliday bound and gagged and dragged off to the hanging tree.

So here he was ...

More than anything, Halliday wanted to wipe the sweat from his face. He caught Joel's eye but the young man stared oddly back at him. Halliday had the feeling that it might pay the young man to remember that Mooney had put a bullet in him, and by Halliday doing what he'd done, had probably saved his life.

A slight measure of hope raised Halliday's spirits. But it was dashed when Nathan lowered his Bible, adjusted his black string tie, and clasped his hands in front of him. His close-set eyes swung around the circle of men but bypassed his daughter and finally settled on Halliday.

"We allow even a murderin' son of a bitch like you a last say, Halliday. Get it over with."

Halliday shook his head and stared incredulously back at him. Nathan eyed him calmly, but Lizzie, adjusting the ribbon so that the neck of her blouse gaped open to display even more of her soft, enticing mounds, said quietly;

"Pa, Buck can't say a word."

"Why in hell not?" Nathan demanded. "He's got a tongue, hasn't he, jest like all of us?"

"It can't operate with that gag in his mouth, pa."

Nathan frowned heavily, then cursed.

"Joel, rip thet gag outta his lyin' mouth."

9

Joel flicked his gun into his right hand and walked lazily toward the hanging tree. He stared into Halliday's eyes while his back was turned toward his father. Then he said with lips barely moving;

"You ride and keep ridin'!"

Halliday was goggle-eyed.

Joel stepped behind him and used his left hand to untie the gag while his right loosened the rope securing Halliday's wrists.

Halliday's fingers closed around Joel's gun butt. Although a surge of relief flooded through him, he kept his eyes on Nathan. When the knot loosened, he spat out the gag. Nathan grunted sourly as Halliday felt the rope around his wrists slacken. He inched his hands apart, shifted Joel's gun from his left hand to his right. Then with a sudden backward step, he elbowed Joel aside and brought the gun up to point squarely at Nathan's head.

As he did so, Lizzie fainted, falling sideways and knocking several men off-balance, her blouse opening fully to expose her creamy breasts.

As if drawn by a magnet, Halliday saw the men's eyes ogle those luscious mounds as he backed away another few paces. His sorrel was tied to the tree and he loosened the reins and swung into the saddle.

"Follow me and I swear to hell, I'll kill you!" Halliday warned. He backed the sorrel up several paces more, then with a sudden dig of his heels, brought it spinning around and heeled it into a run. While the sorrel gathered speed, Halliday heard Nathan shout;

"Get him, dammit! Shoot the lyin' womanizer!"

With Lizzie's breasts still fully exposed, there wasn't a shot to be heard.

It was close to sundown before Buck Halliday stopped to make camp. Thinking back on his short stay in Pardoo only made him angry. The lawman had not only refused to help him, but had cleaned out his pockets and saddlebags, assuring him that where he was going, such items would not be needed.

"Send him to hell and then let us outta here," the man in the middle suggested. "He's nothin' but a thievin' bastard."

Halliday looked at the pile of money scattered on the desktop, then studied Toomey hard.

The lawman shook his head, licked his lips and wiped blood from his head. Halliday wanted to shoot him between the eyes, but so far had refrained from killing crooked lawmen and getting his face on Wanted posters.

"Who are they?" Halliday asked Toomey.

"Scum … of the worst kind. Got word on 'em three days ago and have been waitin' for 'em to show. They robbed the stage depot at Millicent and left behind too many busted heads. When they rode in here, they couldn't wait to take a shot at Ben Cullard's place. They put Ben in the hospital for a week and cleaned out his till. I got word what was goin' on, cornered 'em and brought 'em here. They go to trial in the mornin' … afore they hang."

"Lyin' bastard," came a snarl from the cell. "We didn't do one damn thing he says, mister. He's got us mixed up with some other trio."

Halliday ignored their protests and kept studying Toomey, who now picked up a handful of bills and waved them under Halliday's nose.

"A full day's takin's of around two hundred dollars — which Ben says would be about right, give or take seventy dollars odd that's yours, Mr. Halliday. Ben's gonna lay charges soon as he's back on his feet."

Halliday removed his gun from Toomey's neck and walked across to the cells, then asked the three men;

"What's your story?"

The man in the middle was the tallest and heaviest, a redhead whose hair and beard were thick with grime. He wore a grubby shirt, badly worn Levi's and scuffed boots. There was a scar down his left cheek and his mouth was little more than a ragged gash in a mean-featured face. The other two were smaller but neither had the bigger man's grit.

Halliday built a fire for no other reason than to be able to listen to the crackling of dried timber. He stretched out, feeling the loneliness of the hills close in around him, and tried to sleep. But the more he thought about Sheriff Tad Toomey, the more his anger rose. With no money, no food and only Joel's gun with which to hunt, he knew that Pardoo had profited more from his brief stay than Halliday had.

After twenty minutes of sleeplessness, he rose, kicked dust over the fire and saddled his sorrel. A half-hour later he was out of the foothills and on the trail back to Pardoo. After another hour, he was tying the sorrel to the fence behind the jailhouse. He checked the gun's chambers and found them empty. But he was relieved, knowing that he hadn't ridden into strange country with no means of defending himself.

Keeping the gun in his hand, he quietly climbed the back steps of the jailhouse and tried the door. When the knob turned, he eased the door open and looked inside. Toomey was sitting at his desk, absorbed in counting a bundle of crumpled bills … Halliday's bills.

Halliday quietly made his way up behind the lawman and pressed Joel's empty gun barrel hard against Toomey's neck. The sheriff froze, dropped the money on the desktop, then slowly turned his head.

Halliday then slipped Toomey's gun from its holster and threw it across the room.

"They didn't get to hang me, you shyster."

Sweat broke out on Toomey's brow, his eyes filled with fear. "I told 'em what they planned to do was wrong."

Halliday hit Toomey a glancing blow across the head with the gun sight, and when the lawman cried out in pain, a voice from across the room growled;

"Shoot the bastard, mister, just for the hell of it."

Color drained from Toomey's face as Halliday pushed the gun against his forehead and looked for the speaker. He found not one man, but three rough-looking individuals standing behind the locked bars of a cell.

"Fin Cobb Blaney," the redhead said, nodding at the other two. Mud Drury and Al Lampert. You can look through lawmen's files for a year you won't find our faces on one true bill, Halliday. We rode through Millicent, sure, but we didn't stay longer than to water our horses and to have a drink with an old man there. When we left him, he was sad to see us go."

"You didn't beat him up and rob him?" Halliday asked them quietly.

Blaney rolled his eyes in exasperation. "Rob him! He was a kindly old man makin' his way in a tough world. Why would we want to rob him?"

"For his money," Halliday said simply.

Blaney rolled his eyes again. "An old man like him? What do you take us for, Halliday?"

"I'm yet to make up my mind," Halliday told him, and moved back to find Toomey carefully stacking the money and looking as sad as a beaver on dry land.

"Wouldn't get involved in this, I was you, Mr. Halliday," Toomey said thickly. "These are thievin' scum and no mistake. Ben had his head busted open and he's gonna appear in court to identify 'em As for old Jedro Plant up at Millicent — he's so jittery when strangers drop by, he don't do more'n warm the stock of his old rifle. And his boy, Rowley, has grown just as jittery. He can't put two words together without stutterin'. So tell me why in hell old Jedro would feel sad about these polecats leavin' when they broke his arm and whupped young Rowley so bad he couldn't walk for a week?"

Halliday again checked on the men in the cell. The two smaller prisoners had resumed their places on the bunks, but Blaney still stood holding the bars, shaking his head in complete denial of the accusations.

"I've heard everythin' now," he blurted. "This tin star ain't only a liar, he's a damn fool, to boot. I tell you, Halliday, he jumped us, then locked us up here on that trumped up charge. Let us out and we'll go see Cullard together. Then, when we clear ourselves, we'll just come back and collect that money of ours and light out. I want no part of this one-horser or its damfool badge-toter."

Halliday shrugged and returned his attention to Toomey, found the sheriff frowning deeply while he still fingered the money on the desktop. Halliday stepped up to the desk, opened the top drawer and took out his gunbelt. He then strapped it on and held his hand out to Toomey.

When Toomey nervously licked his dry lips and feigned ignorance, Halliday said;

"Seventy-two dollars, a pack of tobacco and some coffee grounds."

Toomey looked into Halliday's hard eyes. What he saw were the eyes of a man whose patience had run out and who held a gun within an inch of his head. He took some bills from the pile of money and held them out to Halliday. Halliday counted the greenbacks, stuffed them in the pocket of his pants, then turned and tossed Joel's gun at the cell's bars.

While Blaney was trying to catch the gun, Halliday asked the sheriff for his tobacco and coffee, which Toomey took from the second drawer of the desk.

Halliday was about to leave when Blaney pushed the gun through the bars and snarled;

"Okay, Halliday, we're mighty obliged, and we sure hate to do this to a friend. But you best drop that gunbelt, clean out your pockets and don't do nothin' that might cause me to pull this trigger."

Drury and Lampert were grinning like cats that licked the cream as they slapped Blaney on the back. But their smiles quickly disappeared when Halliday said;

"Go jump, Blaney."

For a moment, Blaney's face registered total surprise, then he thumbed back the hammer of the gun and his lips peeled back in a snarl from his yellow teeth when he said;

"You asked for it!"

Toomey cried out when he saw Blaney's finger tighten on the trigger. But when the hammer fell on an empty chamber, he half-rose and stared open-mouthed at Halliday, who said;

"See young Joel gets his empty gun back, will you, Sheriff? Meantime, I'll tie you up so I can leave your peaceable town quietly. Just don't try to follow me or I'll remember that you allowed fools to take the law into their own hands and near had me dance rope."

Toomey's face was ashine with blood and more sweat now as he slumped back into his chair. Halliday rummaged through a pile of gear on the other side of the room that had to belong to the three men in the cell, and found two pieces of rope. He tied Toomey to his chair, then headed for the back door.

Blaney drew his arm back, and with a vile curse, hurled the unloaded gun at Halliday. The gun hit the wall and fell harmlessly to the floor. Halliday picked it up, put it behind his belt and said;

"Enjoy the company, Sheriff."

"Damn you to hell, Halliday!" Toomey growled.

Halliday patted the lawman on the shoulder and left. Just to satisfy his curiosity, he led his sorrel to the yard behind the saloon where he tethered it and walked in to find a short, fat man behind Cullard's counter. Some of the customers recognized him and he heard their whispered comments. But since none of the customers were Nathan Coglan, Joel or any of their friends, he left the saloon and again led his horse up the street.

He crossed the rutted street, leaving his sorrel outside Doc Shaw's cottage, went up the path to the porch and knocked on the front door. When it opened, a wizened face peered out at him.

"How's Ben, Doc?" Halliday asked.

"He'll be fine," the medic answered.

"Hear he was robbed and got his head split open," Halliday said.

"He sure did." The medic's stare became intense. "You're Halliday, aren't you?"

"That's me. Ben know the fellers who jumped him?"

"Wants to get out of bed and identify them." He cleared his throat and added, "How's your neck, Halliday?"

"Not a stretch mark to be seen, Doc."

Halliday left the medic staring curiously at him as he made his way back to the street again. This time, he swung into the saddle and rode back to the jailhouse. From the saddle, he looked in through the jailhouse's front window, saw Toomey still roped to his chair and Blaney was still standing in his cell with his fingers tightly gripping the bars, the knuckles white.

Halliday heeled his sorrel into a run, determined that this time he would not be back. He

19

rode until he came to a fork in the trail where he stopped. Wondering if he had tied up all the loose ends, he finally had to admit to himself that there was one end that he had left undone. He took the south fork and rode for another hour before he drew rein.

Across a clearing, there was a bunkhouse to his right, a large house to his left, and stables in the middle. Halliday headed for the house, left his sorrel tethered at the side and walked around to the back.

As far as he could see, there was only one lamp burning in the house and this was in a room that overlooked the back yard. Halliday stepped up onto the porch, quietly walked down to the lighted window and looked in.

A young woman was sitting on the edge of her bed, brushing her long black hair. Each sweep of her arm seemed to add to the luster of her silky tresses which shone in the light like burnished copper. Halliday watched her for a moment before he tapped lightly on the window glass.

Although it was late and the house was quiet, the woman stared across at him curiously without any sign of surprise or alarm. She stopped her brushing, straightened her blouse, rose and pointed to the door. Halliday walked along the narrow porch and entered through an unlocked rear door.

"Thought you'd be far away by now, Buck," Lizzie said.

Halliday checked the rooms further down the passageway and found there was no light or sound coming from any of them.

"Had some of my things I needed to retrieve in town," he said, entering Lizzie's bedroom.

"Such as?"

"Everyday things … a gun, coffee, tobacco and my money. The sheriff was very obliging, understandably."

Lizzie looked surprised. "You saw Tad Toomey?"

"Just wanted to say goodbye."

Lizzie stood holding her blouse across her chest while the light penetrated her flimsy undergarment, outlining her shapely legs and rounded hips.

Halliday walked across to her as Lizzie's hands dropped to her sides. Then she asked coyly;

"If you got your everyday things back, Buck, why are you here?"

Halliday removed Joel's gun from behind his belt.

"Figured your brother might need this one day."

"Is that the only reason?" Lizzie asked, her tongue moistening her sensual lips.

Halliday unbuckled his gunbelt and hung it over the back of a chair. Then he sat on the side of the bed and removed his boots. Lizzie's eyes gleamed with excitement as she walked provocatively to the bed, undid his pants belt and whispered quietly;

"Just don't wake pa, Buck ... he might not understand."

Halliday had no intention of doing that. He removed his shirt and Lizzie's hands explored his back and then his shoulders. Then he pulled her hard against him.

Lizzie surprised him with the depths of her passion — her young body was warm and lush and for awhile they drifted blissfully in a world of their own.

Then Halliday heard the sound of approaching footsteps outside on the porch. Motioning Lizzie to be silent, he quickly dressed, buckled on his gunbelt, and with Joel's empty gun in his hand, opened the door.

If it was Lizzie's father outside, he figured a smack in the mouth with the gun-loaded fist would be exactly what the man deserved. But when he walked down the passageway and stepped out onto the porch, he saw Joel coming toward him.

The light from Lizzie's room was strong enough to reveal Joel's heavy scowl. When he stopped, hands slack by his sides, and took a look at Lizzie's lighted window, Halliday handed him his gun and said;

"I believe this is yours."

He stepped past Joel and calmly walked to his horse. He was in the saddle when the lamp in Lizzie's room was finally extinguished.

"What in hell's been goin' on, Halliday?" Joel asked.

Halliday smiled and turned the sorrel away from the porch, then said;

"It was more like heaven ..."

He heeled the sorrel into a run, and as he rode away, he heard a curse then the clicks of a gun hammer on empty chambers. He figured Joel would one day soon get himself into a heap of trouble if he didn't put some bullets into that gun of his.

TWO

MOUNTAIN AIR

Buck Halliday rode for three days, living on coffee and jerky before he came to a waterhole where he found jackrabbit spoor. He made camp two hundred yards from the waterhole and unsaddled his sorrel, and by the late afternoon, made his way cautiously back to where he'd seen the sign. There he made a brush hide for himself and settled down to wait. It was just on sundown when two rabbits came warily down to the water. He waited until they were sure it was safe to drink, then took careful aim.

He skinned the rabbits and returned to camp, and within twenty minutes, the rabbits were skewered on a stick and roasting over a fire. The wind rustled through the trees nearby and the last sunlight of the day cast shadows onto the still surface of the waterhole. Halliday figured there couldn't be a better place to spend the evening.

The sharp snap of a stick behind him, followed by the heavy crunch of gravel under a boot, caused him to turn.

He found himself looking into the barrel of an old rifle held by a massive man of indeterminate age. In addition to the rifle, the man held a hatchet in his left hand and there was a knife stuck into the buffalo-hide belt which held up his trousers. A fringed, hide jacket, decorated with porcupine quills, hung down almost to the calf-high top of his deerskin boots.

Halliday knew he was staring, but couldn't help it. Then the man said;

"You ain't Doban."

"You got that right, mister."

"Then who the hell are you?"

When Halliday told him his name, the man lifted his head and his coal-black eyes swept the country about them before coming back to settle on the rabbits cooking over the fire.

"You seen Doban then?"

"I haven't seen a soul in three days."

The man again studied the surrounding countryside, finally looking intently at the steep, boulder-studded country beyond the waterhole, and growled;

"Damn his no-good hide! When we find him, we'll skin him alive then use his carcass to trap bear."

"We?" Halliday asked, remaining seated because he feared this mountain of a man might suddenly lose control of himself and pull the timbered slope down on top of him.

"Six of us — three men and three women."

Halliday put another stick on the fire, then asked;

"I take it Doban's not one of the three?"

The man's eyes were almost lost under his bushy brows as he squinted.

"Was … ain't no more. You ain't, neither, but if you team up with him, we'll skin you, too."

Halliday raised his hands in a gesture of neutrality.

"I'm just driftin' around and mindin' my own business. Soon's I've had somethin' to eat, I'll be on my way."

The man leveled his rifle again and lifted the hatchet to shoulder height.

"And tell Doban where we're at, huh?"

Halliday rubbed his hand lazily across the back of his neck. He shook his head, trying to maintain his composure.

"No, I won't tell him any such thing, won't even talk to him. You want him, go find him. Just leave me out of it."

The brush behind the man parted and a tall, thin man in identical garb stepped out. He had a rifle and a knife, but no hatchet. And just as he lifted his rifle to level it on Halliday, a third man materialized out of the trees up the slope. Halliday studied each man in turn, and asked;

"Maybe I shouldn't wait for these rabbits to cook, eh?"

"You stay put, mister," the thin man said as his companion came down from the slope to tower over Halliday.

As Halliday lifted his arms submissively again, the thin man cracked the barrel of his rifle across his knuckles. When Halliday cried out in protest, the man put his rifle against Halliday's forehead and said;

"I'm for not believin' you, mister."

"What part don't you believe?" Halliday asked, angrily.

"'Bout you not knowin' Doban and not workin' in cahoots with him. Didn't we follow your tracks down here and catch you red-handed?"

"Caught me doing what?" Halliday asked.

The man pointed to the rabbits. "Poachin' and lyin'."

27

"Poaching?" Halliday repeated, stunned by the accusation. As far as he could see, this was open country with no fences, no branded cattle, no mavericks and not a homestead in sight. In fact, for three days he hadn't seen as much as a hoofmark. He rubbed his knuckles and eyed the tall man carefully, then pointed to the fire.

"They're only skinny little rabbits which will make the only hot meal I've had in the three days since I left Pardoo."

"Another lie," the man said and grazed Halliday's forehead with the end of the rifle barrel.

This time, Halliday decided that sitting down wasn't doing him any good, so he came quickly to his feet, careful not to put his hands anywhere near his gun butt. With the gun no longer pressed to his forehead, he felt a lot calmer. He said to the man;

"For hell's sake, put a tie-rope on your friend and let's talk this out."

The man lowered his rifle and the thin man did likewise. But the third man, bulkier than the other two and younger, stood scowling, clearly subservient but straining at the bit for a piece of the action.

"Talk might help, Halliday, so you start."

Halliday felt the man's stare burning into his flesh. He had the uncomfortable feeling that the trio would prefer to eat him rather than the rabbits.

"What do you want to know?" Halliday asked, trying to sound casual, although he was aware that the thin man and the youngest of the trio were now studying him with open hostility.

"Everythin' about you," the man said.

"From when I came here?"

"From the beginnin'," the man said. "Your life story."

Halliday scowled. "What in hell's my past got to do with you finding Doban?"

"It might turn out that we won't need Doban," the man said.

Halliday's stare went from one man to the other, and for the first time, he noticed that the younger and bulkier of the trio resembled the giant in many ways, mainly in the set of his heavy eyebrows and deep-sunken eyes. He wondered if they were related. The other man bore no resemblance to either of other two, except that he was sour-bellied and full of sass.

"How come you suddenly changed your mind about lookin' for Doban? When you came up on me, you sounded ready to tear his head off his shoulders."

"We could still do that," the man assured him. "Only, why should we waste time if he's cleared out? Doban's gutless or he would've stayed and joined our bunch."

"What bunch?" Halliday found himself asking.

The trio appeared to be suddenly overcome by impatience again.

"You want to know a whole lot, Halliday, don't you, for a man trespassin', poachin' and lyin'?"

"Why don't we just kill him?" the younger man asked. "Ain't no place Doban can go, and when he gets hungry, he'll have to come back. So why do we need this uppity jasper, who won't fit in?"

"Fit into what, dammit?" Halliday asked sharply, getting sick of listening to their threats.

The younger man's lips peeled back savagely and he took two quick steps in Halliday's direction. Seeing his knuckles whiten as his grip on his rifle tightened, Halliday dropped his hands to his sides and assumed an air of complete submission.

"Damn nosy, ornery and no-ways neighborly," the young man snarled, and tried to grab Halliday by the throat.

But Halliday had been in too many tight corners and faced greater odds than three against one to let things develop beyond the point where he couldn't handle them.

His left fist slammed resoundingly into the young man's iron-hard stomach and his right hand rose to grab his powerfully-muscled wrist. When the body blow seemed to have little effect, Halliday pulled the wrist down, jerking the man off-balance, then head-butted him under the jaw. The man's reaction was little more than a grunt and Halliday shot a quick look at the others to see them both leering as if they expected to witness a bug being squashed under a boot.

Turning back to his adversary, Halliday was grateful to see a trickle of blood coming from the man's lower lip and this, combined with the confused look in the man's eyes, told Halliday that he'd been hurt. He said;

"None of this is necessary, mister. I haven't anythin' to do with Doban, and don't aim to take on any job he skipped out on. You go your way and I'll go mine."

"He might have what it takes," the giant said quietly. "Don't bruise him too much, Jase."

"Kinda quick," said the tall, scrawny man, and Halliday was positive he detected begrudging praise in his thick, rough-edged voice.

Then Jase, with a nod from the giant, threw his rifle aside and came in. He pushed out a brawny arm which Halliday easily avoided. But Jase brought his arm back, holding his hand against

31

Halliday's head as if measuring him off for the telling blow. Halliday again knocked the arm aside, but when he tried to go in under it, the arm came down on his shoulder like a hammer.

Halliday felt his knees buckle. Then Jase's other hand seized him by the hair and Halliday felt his scalp tighten. As pain tore through his head, Halliday realized he was no match for the man's strength, and decided to try cunning instead. He let his body go limp, and even when Jase's strong fingers held him upright by the roots of his hair, he suppressed the urge to cry out.

"He's a weak 'un," he heard the big youth grumble, then suddenly he was thrown aside.

When Halliday hit the hard ground, he rolled onto his stomach and checked his bearings. He saw he was close to the fire and Jase's rifle on the ground beyond it. His own gun was still in its holster, but Halliday felt that any move he made for it could only spell disaster.

"Damn shame," he heard the giant say. "If he'd measured up, we wouldn't have need of Doban. We could just hunt him down and kill him. Then we could teach Halliday the rules and introduce him to the womenfolk."

Halliday heard footsteps coming up behind him, but before he could turn around, a hand fell on his shoulder and he felt himself being lifted off the ground.

"So kill him," the giant said again. "Can't risk him tellin' anyone about us."

Halliday knew then that staying submissive had been a mistake. As the fingers tightened on his shoulder, he suddenly whipped around and drove his fingertips into Jase's eyes. As Jase released his hold and staggered, Halliday went after him, smashing punch after punch into his face.

Jase's nose was flattened and spurts of blood came from a gashed eyebrow and a split lip, but despite all this, he remained on his feet, not retreating a step or emitting any cry of pain. Then with bruised knuckles and aching limbs, Halliday wondered if the big man was capable of feeling pain.

Neither the giant nor the skinny one had made any attempt to interfere, so Halliday stepped back and looked around for them. He saw the giant leaning on his rifle, grinning, while the skinny man was completely absorbed in studying Jase's injuries. Neither man seemed remotely interested in Halliday.

Halliday drew his gun and leveled it on the giant, bringing a frown and a reproving shake of the head from the man, who muttered;

"No need for that, Halliday."

"Like hell there isn't," Halliday countered. "You crazy bunch of bastards better keep away from me. I'm gettin' on my horse and ridin' out of here. Try to stop me and I'll kill you."

The giant looked at the thin man, who calmly took two steps behind Jase and picked up his rifle. As he turned it in his hands, inspecting it, he said;

"Won't do nobody any good killin' him, will it, Rufe?"

"Can't see as it will," Rufe returned. "But we cain't let him ride out either, Aldo."

"Sure cain't," Aldo said and he leveled the rifle on Halliday. In the meantime, Jase had wiped the blood from his face and stood staring calmly at Halliday. There was no trace of bitterness in his eyes and Halliday had the feeling that he'd soon wake up and this whole nightmare would be a bad dream. Then Rufe lifted his rifle to his shoulder and announced;

"You might get off one shot, Halliday, before we blast you to kingdom come. So you got no way of winnin', have you?"

"I'll take my chances," Halliday replied, and took three careful steps toward the fire.

He leaned down, grabbed the stick holding the rabbits and edged back toward his sorrel.

Neither Aldo nor Rufe made a move to stop him, but their rifles were still aimed squarely at him.

Halliday pushed the rabbits into his saddle-bag, unhitched the sorrel and brought it around to face them. Then he lifted his saddle and saddlebags from the ground and slapped them on the horse's back.

So far so good, he thought, but he knew that when he started to strap on the saddle, both his hands would be occupied and they could easily go for him then.

"We're three men and three women," Rufe announced suddenly, and pointed to Jase. "My son, myself, Jase's three sisters, and Aldo, who's hurt bad and can't help us no more. So we need you, Halliday, for a few months, and you can go on your way if you like with enough pelts, hides and gold to keep you in comfort for the rest of your days. What do you say?"

Halliday shook his head and moved his gun into his left hand. Then he reached under the sorrel's belly and pulled the girth tight. He studied Aldo and Rufe carefully again, then decided to take a chance. But before he could finish buckling the strap, Rufe sighed sorrowfully and spoke again;

"Nothin' for it then, Halliday, but to let you think on it. But while you're lookin' for a way outta this valley, make sure you don't let Doban hurt you. He's kill-crazy."

"And you're not?" Halliday shot back at him.

Rufe shook his head. "We're just normal people who've staked our claim to this valley and mean to hold onto it, no matter what. Doban could have joined us, but had ideas of his own, tried to rob us, then lit out to escape punishment. But like you'll find out when you leave here, he's got no place to go and sooner or later, he'll have to come back to us. That's when we'll kill him."

Halliday again looked to the land beyond the waterhole. The eerie silence made him feel uneasy.

"Maybe I won't go," he said, stalling for time, unsure if Aldo was completely subservient to Rufe's authority. "Maybe I'll go back."

Rufe shook his head again. "We won't allow you to do that, Halliday. Jase and Aldo will be camped on the trail you used to get here. You won't get by them, just as Doban won't. So what's ahead of you is hidin' out in that country up there with a kill-crazy man likely breathin' down your neck. Either he'll get you or you can throw in with us. On our terms."

"What terms?" Halliday asked.

Rufe again shook his head. "You're not in the right frame of mind right now, Halliday. Mebbe in a week. Now go."

Halliday moved the sorrel back a little more, giving himself as much cover as possible. When none of the three made a move to stop him, he stepped up into the saddle. The top of his head still felt as if it had been scalped and his shoulder, where Jase's huge hand had gripped him, felt bruised. But apart from that, he felt capable of handling anything else they might start.

He backed the sorrel away while watching the three men intently. But when he made a sudden shift to the right, Jase moved to block his way. A shift to the left brought the same response from Aldo. Rufe merely stood his ground, sighing wearily, his rifle leaning against his thigh. He said;

"Straight past the waterhole, Halliday. When you've had enough, come back here and we'll take you home."

Halliday rubbed his hand roughly across the back of his neck, more than eager to see the last of them. However, he had the feeling that before he had ridden fifty feet, he would be cut down.

He rode toward a huge boulder to the left of the waterhole, letting the sorrel set its own pace before suddenly dropping down on its neck and kicking it into a run.

He cut across open country for a hundred yards without a shot being fired, then rode the sorrel hard up a steep slope into heavily-timbered country. Only when he was out of six-gun range did he slow down and look back.

There was no sign that the trio planned to follow him. He sat his horse and pondered his fate. He'd heard about people like that trio — hillbillies who inbred and lived a life of their own. He wondered how in hell he'd landed in such a mess.

Somehow, he had left a well-used trail and had strayed into this godforsaken valley. But if there was a way in, there had to be a way out. He swung to the ground, tightened the cinch a notch, then led his sorrel to the rim of the slope.

There, for the first time, he could see the valley, for what it was worth. And it didn't look to be worth much. Rocky cliffs brooded down on grassless slopes that were studded with enough boulders to construct a dozen fortresses high enough that no man, not even Rufe, could scale.

He decided to make camp, now that night was closing in around him, eat his rabbits and get as much rest as he could, then be gone before sunup.

With caution uppermost in his mind, he sought out a cleared space between several towering boulders. He ground hitched the sorrel, spread his blanket out, took the rabbits from the saddlebag and squatted down to eat.

He had swallowed one mouthful when a rush of footsteps came from behind him and before he could turn, a huge shadow loomed over him. Above it, he saw the blurred outline of a branch coming toward his head. He threw himself to one side and the branch swished past his ear. Before he could collect his senses, the huge shadow had materialized into the hulking figure of a man who looked more animal than human.

Halliday's rabbits were scooped from the blanket, and before he could protest or draw his gun, the man, who Halliday guessed had to be Doban, bounded back behind the boulders and was gone.

Halliday recovered from his shock and gave chase, but by the time he had skirted the boulders, the man was going over the top of a steep rise, his tattered coat flapping in the breeze and his matted hair streaming out behind him.

Cursing, Halliday slowly made his way up until he stood staring down at another sweep of rugged slopes which led onto the most desolate stretch of desert he had ever seen. The sky above it was completely cloudless and there was no sound to be heard but the light whisper of the wind through the gaunt, barkless trees and clusters of sun-bleached boulders.

He inspected the ground until he picked up the trail of his visitor. He followed it along the ridge line until he saw the mouth of a cave set back in the rocky cliff face. Approaching cautiously, he drew his gun, waited, and when no sound came from within the cave, quietly closed in.

He was within ten paces of the mouth of the cave when a barrage of rocks came hurtling out at him. Struck on the side of the head, on his left shoulder and finally on the chest, Halliday backed off and found cover behind a deadfall. But no sooner had he done so than the hulking shape of a man burst from the cave and went rushing along the ridge line away from him.

Halliday leveled his gun on the man and punched off one shot. He heard the bullet hit home but the big man's stride didn't falter. In fact, if anything, it lengthened. Halliday took off after him, but although he was swift-footed and driven by a burning desire to get his hands around the man's neck, by the time he reached the ridge line, he was alone again.

He leaned against a boulder and mopped sweat from his brow and neck. Silence settled again and with darkness closing in, he figured further searching would be futile. He retraced his steps to where he had hitched his sorrel only to find it had gone. To add to his misery, his blanket was missing as well.

Cursing again, he studied the ground for sign and discovered the prints of two men. Consumed with anger, he strode down the slope in the direction of the waterhole but was still within a hundred yards of it when a bullet from a rifle whistled past his ear. Then he heard Rufe shout;

"You'll need all the rest you can for the days ahead, Halliday, so why not get it? Steer clear of Doban or he'll kill you and keep away from this water or we'll do the same."

"Crazy bastards!" Halliday shouted back.

"Rest and put your mind at ease. Within a few days, when you're thirsty and your gut is crying out for food, come back here to us. You'll find us only too willin' to help."

"If I get a bead on any of you, I won't be askin' for any help," Halliday threatened.

"Two, three days," was the quiet reply across the heat-choked valley.

41

Then Halliday saw Rufe's tall figure walking away from the waterhole. He swung his gaze up to the high country beyond and saw two figures standing fifty yards apart, rifles across their chests. Beyond them was the trail that had brought him into this valley. He rubbed his chest where one of Doban's rocks had struck him and decided there was nothing else to do but some long, hard thinking.

This was one hell of a crazy situation.

THREE

UNUSUAL ALLY

Among other things, Jake Doban was a puzzled man. He had come to accept near-starvation, a three-day thirst, a bullet wound in his side and a burning desire for revenge. But despite all these troubles, he couldn't get the arrival of the new man out of his mind.

He'd heard him say his name was Buck Halliday, then had seen him stand up to Rufe Masterson and his son and the beanpole, Aldo Cobbitt.

Doban disregarded the fact that he had been forced to rob Halliday of his supper. He knew now that he needed Halliday and Halliday needed him.

How else would he get past Jase and Aldo, take Mercy away from her father and escape to freedom?

He decided he would have to make a deal with Halliday and try to enlist his help.

Crunching the rabbit between his teeth, Doban finished his meal, but even while he licked his fingers clean, he still felt hungry. For the last three days, he had eaten nothing but grass and moistened his dry lips and throat with cactus juice. He felt his strength ebbing away and knew he would never be a match for the powerful Jase Masterson.

If he could only get his hands on Halliday's gun, he felt he could kill the trio and rescue his beloved girl. Then he would set the others free but they would have to cope on their own. They were devoted to their father and unconditionally obeyed his orders, agreeing with his crazy plan without argument.

Slatterns, Doban decided. Even when he'd first been captured and taken to their camp and was forced to watch them parade naked in the raw sunlight, he had been unimpressed. But Mercy had captured his interest. She was all he wanted. With a fair share of Masterson's pelts, and some of his gold as a dowry, he figured they could light out and head for a better life. And Mercy had intimated that she would go along with any scheme he thought up as long as they escaped. Even if it meant he would have to shoot his way out of the valley prison.

Prison …?

What else could anybody call a place where Rufe ruled like a tyrant, where the dim-witted Jase watched their every move, where Aldo hated him because he couldn't make it with the women anymore.

And Mercy's sisters …?

They kept staring at him as if he were a prize bull.

Doban wiped sweat from his brow. He'd never been much of a lady's man, not since his first effort with that saloon whore in Toledo after which she'd ridiculed him for his inexperience.

Doban brooded and scowled into the night around him. It was still hot, but the heat was having little affect on him. He had put all thoughts of discomfort from his mind, knowing that he would have to make plans.

Cobbitt and Jase controlled the waterhole and would shoot anybody who came near it. Day and night, one of them was always on guard. They were dominated by Rufe and would die rather than fail him. Rufe himself stayed with the women, and had convinced the two older sisters,

Charity and Glory, that Mercy's weakness in wanting to leave with Doban was due totally to her innocence.

Doban knew that the reason Mercy had not sought him out was because the others were watching her every minute of the day.

And all that, he told himself, was what he was up against — murdering scum, a demented old man, three women held captive under the spell of a social outcast.

To combat them, Doban had failing strength, starvation and a tongue so swollen from lack of water he was hardly able to raise a spit, even if the necessity arose. Added to this was the wound in his side, inflicted by the newcomer, Buck Halliday.

Halliday!

Doban brought his straying thoughts into focus. Halliday had a gun and he was tough and shrewd. Doban had realized as much while hiding when he had witnessed the set-to with Jase. So there were actually two of them now who had to fight their way out of this prison. If he could only gain Halliday's confidence and they combined forces, surely one of them could get through.

And Doban knew who that one would be.

He'd get a horse, water, provisions and ride out. When he had regained his strength, he'd sneak back to rescue Mercy.

He smiled as he thought of her. She was all woman — young, desirable and passionate. From the first moment they had seen each other, he had been attracted to her and knew she felt the same about him. But the others had kept them apart. Rufe had made him help Jase and Aldo build three separate cabins, one for each of the sisters, while the men lived in a communal cabin. There'd been talk about Doban marrying all three. Doban was sure that if he got the sisters pregnant, he would no longer be needed, and they would most likely dispose of him.

Rufe's plan to build a new community and stock it with his own people did not include any outsiders. Nor would they let him leave to spread the word about what they were doing.

They would get rid of him, trap another unsuspecting drifter, and go through the procedure again.

Sweat beaded his brow when he thought of his last night in camp. Weary to the point of exhaustion, he had retired to the cabin they had allotted him, and as he was dozing off, had overheard raised voices. That same day the last of the cabins had been completed, and as in the construction of the other two, he had done most of the heavy lifting. He had been so weary, he couldn't keep his eyes open. Later, wakened from a deep sleep, it had taken him some time to realize that Mercy was lying beside him.

Cautioning him to stay quiet, she had told him that all the rituals leading up to the wedding ceremonies would begin the next morning, and she wasn't sure if she wanted to share him with her sisters.

Roused by her warm and willing body, Doban had decided to reap some reward for all his efforts when Rufe had stormed in, thrown Mercy out, and with Aldo and Jase, had proceeded to beat him within an inch of his life.

Doban had managed to escape and had headed for the desolate section of the valley. For two days, he had hidden out while recovering from the beating. He hadn't seen Mercy since, and just that morning before Halliday's arrival, he had almost been caught when he was within sight of the waterhole. As he retreated back to his refuge, Rufe had yelled at him that Mercy no longer wanted him and he would have to die.

Doban rubbed his hands down the thick hair on his chest and looked into the starlit sky, wondering when it was going to rain. He recollected that on the few occasions he'd been allowed to leave the camp to cut timber for the cabins, he'd been surprised by the lush richness of the country south of camp. It was the most beautiful valley he had ever seen, and although Rufe had hinted that he might be allowed to stay on and become one of the family, he was warned that this section was strictly off-limits.

He hadn't argued because at the camp there was plenty of food and all the water he needed. He had shelter in this out-of-the-way place. Sure, he would have liked something stronger, and maybe some companionship, but then there was Mercy, touching his hand and glancing at him when the others weren't looking, hinting that their time to be together would come soon.

Doban clambered to his feet, feeling aches in every bone. His stomach craved for food and his throat was parched. He knew he couldn't last another day and that tonight he must do something. He crawled out of his cave and crept to the edge of the ridge. Since he'd heard the rifle shot which had forced Halliday to pull back from the waterhole, everything had been quiet.

But he knew Jase and Aldo were standing guard and would shoot to kill next time. Doban carefully picked his way across the ridge, feeling the dry night air draining the energy from his body. He wanted to lie down and sleep, but sensed that if he did, he might never see another sunrise. So he had to find Halliday.

Halfway down the slope, he stopped suddenly. As always, there was dead quiet from the northern, western and eastern sections where the desert enclosed him. But from the southern section, possibly from the Masterson camp, came a thumping noise. It went on for several minutes before it, too, died and silence settled over the land again. He scratched the dry skin on his neck and stood waiting and listening. Then a call came from below;

"That's far enough, mister. Keep to hell away from me."

Doban glared into the darkness. "Halliday?"

"You figure the population's increased since sundown, Doban?"

"You know me?" Doban queried, warily taking a few more steps.

"I know enough to tell you that if you take another step, I'm going to pull this trigger."

Doban stopped and scowled into the dark.

"We have to talk," he said a moment later, his voice quiet as if he feared being overheard.

"We've got nothing to talk about," Halliday replied.

He came to his feet, remembering that this man had stolen his supper and the Mastersons had stolen his horse. He couldn't sleep for the dryness in his throat and cursed the fact that he had drunk so much whiskey in Pardoo. Added to that, he was hungry, but more than anything, he was riled at not being able to go where he liked, when he liked.

"Sure we have, Halliday. Hell, you've met these people. They're loco. They've had me trapped in this damn oven for three days now with no water or food."

"You ate my rabbits," Halliday reminded him.

"It was either eat them or die. But that country on the other side of the waterhole, maybe you can tell me how come it's the way it is — good country on one side and nothing on the other side but sand, rocks and snakes."

"How the hell should I know?" Halliday snapped.

Doban was silent for a time, rubbing his cracked lips on the back of his hand.

Then he started to approach Halliday again, only to be warned by the sound of a gun hammer being snagged back.

"Listen, they got you in the same fix as they've got me. I've been out here for three days and nights. And I tell you, there ain't no way out except up the track that leads past that water-hole. Like me, you musta missed the trail to Creede and strayed this way. You musta seen the hills, too, eh?"

Halliday admitted that he had. After leaving Lizzie, he hadn't given much thought to where he was going, just so long as he put Pardoo behind him. Riding aimlessly, one moment he had been in prairie country and the next the grass gave out, there were no trees and the wind was like a furnace. So instead of retracing his steps, which had been his intention, he had ridden toward this line of hills. He'd come through a narrow pass and that's when he'd come across the water-hole. He asked;

"What's north and east of here?"

"Sand. And I'm not lyin'. You think I'd have holed-up here with these crazies if there was a way out?"

Halliday thought about that and decided no man would be that stupid.

"Rufe said you tried to rob him."

Doban laughed. "How in hell could anybody do that? Every damn minute of every day and night one of them bastards has a hatchet or rifle trained on me. Even when Rufe uncovers his altar and gathers what he calls his flock around him, there's always one of 'em ready to slip a blade or a bullet in my back if I so much as blinked."

"Rufe also mentioned women," Halliday said quietly.

"There's three of 'em, damned pretty and hog-wild."

"He also offered me pelts, gold and hides — enough to set me up for life."

"I had a similar offer," Doban told him.

"It didn't appeal to you?"

"Some of it did."

"What parts didn't?"

"The deal with the three of them," Doban said.

Halliday frowned. He had already decided that Masterson and his helpers were something out of the ordinary. And from Doban's manner, he didn't consider him to be much better. Or perhaps it was just due to lack of food and water and being hunted like an animal for three days. He asked;

"How about makin' that plainer, mister, and if I can make some sense out of what you say, maybe you can come closer and let me get a better look at you."

"I can only tell you the truth, Halliday, for what it's worth. I strayed this way and somebody came up behind me and knocked me from my saddle. When I came to, three naked women were standin' around me. I figured I'd died an' gone to heaven, except the pain in my head told me I was more likely in hell. Then Rufe came up, sent the women away and Jase and Aldo sat down and questioned me about where I'd come from and why and how I'd come to this valley. I told them exactly as it had happened. I didn't know if they believed me or not, but from then on, I was kept in a cabin sweatin' near to death. But they fed me and gave me plenty of water, so I just bided my time until I could get my horse and light out. On the third day, the three of them came to me again and said I'd been accepted into their family, whatever that might be. All I had to do was read from the Bible every day, sundown and sunup, and help them build cabins for the women. I figured that was all right, kinda like payin' for my keep, so we built three cabins with me doing most of the work. By this time, Rufe had weighed things up and decided I would marry his three daughters —"

"All of them?"

"All three of 'em." Doban gave a hollow laugh. "How about that, eh? Hell, it ain't that I don't fancy women, but havin' three wives and two of 'em damn hard to get on with wasn't my idea of the perfect life. Besides, the youngest, Mercy, was

54

pretty as a picture, and she'd told me she wanted me for herself and that sat all right with me, too. Then the other night, the men busted in on us and near beat me to death. I got away and for the last three days they've hunted me, kept me hungry and dyin' of thirst and bleedin' like a stuck pig."

Halliday leaned back against the warm side of a boulder and licked his lips. At odd times in his life, he'd been so down on his luck that he'd traded all his possessions for a stake, but never had he sold his horse or his gun. Yet right then, he was willing to trade everything he owned for a jug of cold water.

"Why would he force you into marryin' all his daughters?" Halliday wanted to know.

"Because he's crazy, or whatever it is that he's startin' up says all his people have got to be descended from him. So he's using his daughters to start a congregation. Guess he figures if I get all three of them pregnant, he's on his way. But then he wouldn't need me, would he?"

"Women can have more than one child," Halliday informed him.

"But Rufe don't want one father for all his off-spring. He aims to start with me, get rid of me, then bring another drifter in, set him up, then get rid of him, too. Charity and Glory are willin' to go along because he's got them under his thumb. Mercy's against it, that's why she wanted to run away with me."

"What about Jase and Aldo?" Halliday asked.

"Aldo got injured when he was thrown from a hoss two years ago and isn't any good to a woman, he says. Rufe let him stay because he's strong and a good hunter and doesn't do anythin' but what Rufe tells him. He's no threat to the women and can't make trouble for the men."

"And Jase?" Halliday asked.

"He's their brother, ain't he?" Doban threw back. "Hell, they might be crazy, but they don't go along with that kind of thing. But Rufe's got plans for Jase, too, and says just as soon as the women are set up, he'll bring one in for Jase. Naturally, after she's given the congregation a child, she'll have the same fate as me."

"You might be crazy, Doban," Halliday called out to him, "but you aren't dull."

"It's the truth, Halliday," Doban yelled back. "You got to believe me. Think about what they told you. What other answer is there for them letting you go, taking your horse and keeping you confined here except that they're goin' to kill me because I upset Rufe's plans and can't be trusted? I'm tellin' you, they looked you over properly when you were locking horns with Jase

56

and decided you've got what they want. You're big, you ain't stupid, and you ain't bad-lookin'. I can maybe last out the night, then I'll go out of my head and have to make a try for the water-hole. They'll shoot me down like a dog and bide their time until you have to come out of hiding. Then they'll drag you off, fatten you up, intro-duce you to the women and when your duty's done, they'll have no more need for you, either."

Halliday wiped beads of sweat from his brow. He had an uncomfortable feeling that some of what Doban had just said was true. And if all of it was true, then what? He said, quietly;

"You can come closer, Doban, but so help me, don't try to jump me. You haven't got a friend in this valley, so remember it."

A deep grunt of satisfaction came from Doban, then he lumbered across to stand near Halliday and regarded him sullenly.

"You and me," he muttered, "that's our only chance."

In the starlight, Halliday studied him closely, and what he saw sent a shiver down his spine. Not only was Doban's side covered in blood but his face was a mass of welts and bruises. His nose was broken and his cheeks had swollen to link up with his beetling brow so that his eyes were mere slits. His mouth was bruised and split, one shoulder drooped, and his left arm hung limp at his side.

Halliday lowered his gun and whistled softly. "They didn't go easy on you, mister, did they?"

"They're scum. I can take Jase and they know it. Aldo too, given a fair shake. But the three of them were too much for me."

"The women stand by and watch it all happen?" Halliday asked.

"No."

"What about Mercy?"

"There's a lot of Rufe in Mercy."

Halliday came to his feet but made sure to keep away from Doban's huge hands, and stared across at the waterhole. There was not a sound in the valley, and above, the starlit sky was cloudless. Today had been one of the hottest he'd experienced in months and he sensed that tomorrow would be no better.

"You have some idea how to pull it off?" Halliday asked finally.

Doban eyed him enthusiastically. "You're with me then?"

Halliday shrugged and pointed to the country behind him. "One thing I do believe is that if there's a way out of this valley, you'd have found it. And since I don't hanker to stay here any longer than I have to, I'm willin' to buy into any scheme you can come up with."

"They'll be watchin' every minute, waitin' to cut me down. You might be safe because they need you. So what we have to do is have them watchin' you, which will give me time to get past them. Maybe I should have your gun to give me some sort of protection."

Halliday laughed. "And maybe I should start making a marker for my grave."

Doban swore under his breath.

"Well, you come up with something, dammit!" he growled, then fell into a fit of coughing.

Halliday eyed him coldly until the spasm had passed, then he said;

"What I'm not goin' to come up with is givin' you my gun and puttin' my life in your hands. You think I'm a fool?"

"I know you're not. But what other way is there? Jase can shoot the eye out of a chicken hawk and Aldo can split bark from a tree at a hundred paces with his hatchet. As for Rufe, he considers human sacrifice, regardless of who it might be, as a mark in his favor in the Good Book. Then there's the women. They ain't there just to bear kids, they're guardians of the Masterson temple and will tear your eyes out if you don't toe the line."

Doban scrubbed a hand across his misshapen face and his body seemed to sag. Halliday had the strong suspicion the man was pretending to be weaker than he actually was, and took a firmer hold on his gun. He didn't want to shoot the man, but if it meant survival for himself, he wouldn't hesitate. He moved back a couple of paces and again looked down the slope to where the surface of the waterhole gleamed in the starlight.

"Well, what about this idea?" Doban asked a moment later.

He was now down on his haunches and scratching at the ground with a stick. He didn't look at Halliday as he outlined his plan.

"We'll go for each other and make it look like we've finally cracked. I'll start throwin' rocks and you start firin' some bullets. We'll keep circlin' until we work our way in close to the waterhole, but so far apart that whoever's on watch won't know which one of us to take first."

He looked up and his almost buried eyes gleamed with excitement.

"But I got to have more cover than you 'cause it'll be me they'll go after first. You might make it to those rocks beside the waterhole, and from there you can give me cover. We'll at least have water."

The thought of a drink made Halliday lick his lips. He was not surprised to find they were cracked and bleeding. He took another long look at the country between them and the waterhole. Far across on the slope was a cluster of rocks and below them a smaller cluster. In between was a scattering of dead trees and beyond them a huge pile of rocks and deadfalls indicating that there'd once been a landslide on that side of the valley. He believed if he tried Doban's plan under cover of darkness, there was just sufficient cover to give them a chance — but for one thing.

"How long can you stay on your feet?"

Doban eyed him defiantly. "After what I been through, and with what I've got to gain, I'll last a half-hour, maybe longer. I got to get that water and nobody's gonna stop me — not even you."

Halliday put his back to the stump of a tree and studied Doban gravely. It was not yet midnight so they still had plenty of time. Just then a full moon appeared over the horizon and bathed the whole area in light.

Doban cried out in despair, sank to his knees and began to beat his hands on the ground.

Halliday knew that if things weren't so serious the whole affair would be more like one huge, massive joke.

FOUR

JAILBREAK

Nathan Coglan stormed into the Pardoo jail-house to find Sheriff Tad Toomey seated behind his desk, a rifle on the scarred top and a canteen to his lips.

"No time for sittin' around, Tad," Coglan growled. "You got to be up and goin'."

"Goin' where?" Toomey asked.

As usual, he was fearful of Coglan's power and influence, but the day was so hot nothing short of a gunpowder blast was about to move him.

"After Halliday, of course!"

Toomey rolled his eyes and sank deeper into his chair. He lifted the canteen and poured water over his head, letting it drip onto his shirt and down his back.

"Halliday's well gone," he said. "I didn't bat an eye when you dragged him off to hang him but I hear your son slipped a gun to him, allowin' him to get away."

"Halliday got the drop on Joel and don't you say otherwise. He's a no-good, thievin' ne'er-do-well, and the sooner you bring him back and I get to hang him, the better for ev'rybody. You goin' or ain't you?"

Toomey sat forward and pulled a pad toward him, took a pencil from his shirt pocket, licked the end of it and asked;

"What's the complaint?"

"Rape, dammit! What else with a varmint like that?"

Toomey scribbled the word on the pad.

"So, who did he rape?"

Coglan came up to the desk and dropped his gnarled fists on the desktop, leaning forward so his face was within a couple of inches of the lawman's.

"Weren't me, dammit, Tad."

"Who, then?" Toomey asked, sounding more hot and bothered than ever.

Coglan reached forward and grabbed the sheriff by his collar and pulled him across his desk.

"You're rilin' me considerable, damn you!"

"Well, I'm right sorry about that, but we do things by the book around here. Sometimes, anyway."

Coglan let him go and said, quieter, "My little girl's the one. Defiled her, he did. Took her against her will!"

Toomey removed the hand and sleeved sweat from his face, anger showing in his eyes.

"Way I heard it, your daughter went to Halliday's room of her own free will, and when Dace got wind of it, he pulled a gun and came off second best."

"Not that time, dammit!" Coglan snarled, and hammered his fist on the desk. "I'm talking about last night. Trespassin', breakin' and enterin' … and rape!"

Toomey lifted his hand to his mouth to conceal a smile. Halliday was some piece of work. He'd come back, demanded the return of his belongings, tricked the three outlaws in the cells into convicting themselves, and ridden out without batting an eyelid. On his way out, he'd paid a visit to Lizzie. Thinking of the full-breasted young woman, Toomey sighed deeply and muttered; "Lizzie's makin' the complaint then?"

Coglan eyed him ferociously. "She's back on the ranch and she's gonna stay there. Joel's makin' sure Halliday doesn't come back. So get yourself into your saddle and get after him. Drifters don't travel fast, so we should run him down easy."

Toomey threw down the pencil and came to his feet. He stared across the jailhouse to where Cobb Blaney, Jud Drury and Al Lampert were standing in line behind the bars. Earlier that day, Ben Cullard had identified all three as the men who had robbed his saloon and put him under Doc Shaw's care. As soon as the Circuit Judge arrived, Toomey would have them in court.

"What do you reckon I should do with my prisoners while I'm out lookin' for a will-o'-the-wisp like Buck Halliday?" Coglan glared at the three hard cases, then demanded; "Who the hell are they?"

"Three outlaws who robbed Jedro Plant up in Millicent a week ago then rode into town and robbed Ben Cullard. In my opinion, they need my attention more than Halliday does."

"All lies!" Blaney yelled, looking squarely at Coglan and speaking in a softer tone. "Hell, mister, talk to this fool for us, will you? Then, by hell, we'll saddle up and ride with you and run that rapist down. I swear we will."

"Don't listen to them," Toomey said, but Coglan, having thoroughly studied them again, approached the cells and asked; "Ain't horse thieves, are you?"

"No way!" Blaney lied.

"Nor cattle rustlers, I hope?"

Blaney turned his face to the ceiling and rolled his eyes. "We're cowhands and we work hard for our money. We respect the men who opened up this land and made it better for everyone. Why, if it wasn't for ranchers like you, Mr. Coglan —"

"How do you know I'm a rancher?" Coglan shot back at him.

Blaney looked perplexed for a moment, then said;

"Didn't I just now hear you charge a drifter with the rape of your daughter who is back at your ranch with her brother?"

Coglan grunted, then went on with his questioning.

"You ain't outlaws of any kind?"

"I'll swear it on the Bible," Blaney replied innocently.

Coglan eyed him suspiciously, then turned to Toomey.

"I want these men handed over to me, Sheriff."

"You *what?*" Toomey gaped.

"If you don't aim to help, I'm in a desperate situation which demands desperate measures."

He drew his gun and held it on the lawman. "Get your keys, Tad."

Toomey shook his head and backed away. "Don't think you c'n scare me into lettin' them out. I won't forget this, either, you can bet."

His face reddening, Coglan pushed the gun against the sheriff's jaw and forced him back to his desk. Then he grabbed a ring of keys from a wall hook and turned toward the cells. But when Toomey's anger got the better of him and he lunged at the rancher, Coglan hit him across the face with his gun barrel.

"Dammit, Tad, I got to go after Halliday. Can't you see that?"

Toomey couldn't see a thing because his feet had lost contact with the floor and the side of his head had struck the corner of the desk. He fell with blood welling from the gash on his face.

Coglan hurried to the cell and tried key after key in the lock until finally he found one that fitted. The lock clicked open and Coglan pulled the door back. He didn't have time to move out of the way before the trio rushed from the cell, knocking him aside.

Coglan lost his footing and reached out for the bars for support. Then Drury, the smallest and meanest of the bunch, tore the gun from

Coglan's hand and brought it down on the rancher's head, sending him to the floor with a whimper.

Blaney checked the street, then came back to glare down on the sheriff, who was kneeling on the floor now and groaning with his head held between his bloodied hands.

Blaney pulled open the desk drawers until he found their gun rigs. After distributing them and strapping on his gunbelt, he grabbed Toomey by the collar and hauled him across the room, tossing him into their cell, then dragging Coglan in after him. Then he closed and locked the door and removed the keys.

By that time, Drury had searched through the remaining drawers and found the money they had stolen from Cullard the previous night. Stuffing it into his shirt, he joined Lampert at the back door. While Blaney hurried toward them, the semiconscious rancher struggled to his feet, and with blood streaming down his face, shook his fist at them and yelled;

"I'll … get you for this if it takes me … a lifetime. I'll spend every penny I have hirin' men to run you down. There won't be an inch of this territory where you can … hide."

Drury waited until Lampert and Blaney had gone through the back door, then drew his gun and fired off two quick shots at the cells. Both bullets slammed into Coglan's chest, and even as Blaney wheeled away, grabbing Drury and shaking him, the rancher pitched forward onto the cell floor and died.

"You damn fool!" Blaney yelled, his fist drawn back to smash the smaller man to the ground while Lampert raced for the stables. Drury and Blaney looked down the street and saw a bunch of townsmen running toward them with guns drawn.

Blaney pushed Drury down the steps and followed him, and by the time Lampert had saddled his horse, bullets were hammering into the walls around them.

Blaney yelled for Lampert to hold the townsmen off while he and Drury saddled up, but when the shooting became heavier, Lampert kicked his horse into a run and sped down the alley.

Blaney swung into the saddle and heeled his horse away. He had just cleared the yard with a cursing Drury following him when a hail of bullets sounded. Drury was almost knocked from the saddle as a bullet tore through his shoulder, but he managed to hold grimly onto the horse's neck.

Blaney had ridden through the gunfire unscathed and was fast closing in on Lampert, who belatedly began to return fire. Blaney slowed his mount as Lampert came within gun range, then wild-eyed and cursing, he emptied his gun into his partner. When Lampert threw up his arms and pitched from the saddle, Drury thundered past with Blaney following.

By the time they neared the end of the alley, the shooting had ceased, but they still drove their horses hard until they reached the outskirts of town, where Drury slowed to wait for Blaney to catch up to him, then drew his gun. Lifting his own gun in reply, Blaney snarled;

"You want it too, Jud?"

Drury eyed him savagely, his chest heaving when he growled;

"You killed Al!"

"Because he ran out on us … both of us. Dammit, you made a mess o' things back there by shootin' that rancher, but Al turned his back on us. You want to sit here and talk about it or do we get shuck of this town?"

Both hard cases knew it would not be long before somebody released the sheriff from his cell and a posse was formed. Drury nodded and said;

"We'll ride, but so help me, this isn't the end of it. Me and Al rode a lot of trails together."

"This time he was on his own and lookin' after his own skin," Blaney shot back, then whipped his horse into a run again.

As Blaney thundered away, Drury took a last look at the crowd forming in the street ...

"You ready, Halliday?"

Looking no better despite a two-hour sleep, Doban stopped within five paces of Buck Halliday to watch him check his gun. His eyes were almost closed but he kept a close eye on Halliday's every move. Despite the effort it took to concentrate on what was happening, he was waiting for a chance to catch Halliday off his guard, take his gun and kill him.

But the drifter had met desperate men like Jake Doban before. He rose, stretched his arms and rolled his shoulders, then moved back until he was well away from the man.

"There's too much light," he said.

"In another two hours it'll be sunup, and if I don't get water by then, I'm not gonna be able to talk," Doban muttered.

Even now, his voice came raspingly from his swollen mouth and his breathing sounded tortured.

Halliday checked the country ahead once again. Nothing had changed to encourage him to undertake this attempt to run the gauntlet of Jase Masterson and Aldo Cobbitt's gunfire. Yet he knew that if he didn't try something, Doban would soon go out of his mind and might even attack him.

"Which way do you want to go?" Halliday asked.

Doban's body shook and his arms hung limply by his sides.

"I'll go for that cluster of rocks to the right. If they start firin' at me, give me cover."

Despite the man's confidence that the Mastersons would spare him, Halliday had other ideas. The main one being that these fools couldn't possibly expect any stranger to fall in with their plans of marriage and confinement to this valley. So they'd gun him down, just as they'd gun Doban down.

"Whenever you're ready," Halliday said.

Doban nodded, managed to stop shaking, then went into a crouch. Pushing himself off the ground, he suddenly leaped forward and broke into a staggering run. Halliday watched him closely, and just when he seemed likely to reach the protective cover of some boulders, rifle fire from two different directions broke the night's stillness, sending Doban to the ground.

Halliday drew his gun, jumped to his feet and broke from cover, firing first at one muzzle flash, then at the other. He had gone fifty yards before the first bullet sought him out. This was no more than a warning as dirt spurted from the ground ten feet in front of him.

Choking back a curse, Halliday kept running. Two bullets whistled past his head before Jase's voice boomed above the echoes of the gunshots.

"You got no chance, Halliday. Stay put!"

Halliday saw that he was only twenty yards from the first boulder and kept going. But after two more strides, he veered to the left, went another five strides, then veered back. Bullets zipped all around him now as he went into a dive.

He hit the ground five feet in front of the boulder and rolled the rest of the way, keeping his gun clamped to his chest. When he reached safety, he quickly came to his haunches. Jase and Aldo peppered the face of the biggest boulder with rifle fire. Then a deep silence filled the valley again.

Halliday reloaded his six-gun and looked across to where he'd seen Doban go down. To his surprise, the massively-built man was struggling to his feet. Doban lifted his fist into the air and cursed wildly, but when he started to limp toward the waterhole, fresh gunfire broke out. Halliday saw Doban's body jerk and reel until finally he went down on his knees again. He swayed back and forth, his bulky body clearly visible in the moonlight until a final shot blew his face away.

Halliday sleeved sweat from his face and tried to swallow. He knew he had in some way caused the man's death because he hadn't tried hard enough to talk him out of his crazy plan. Instead, he'd used Doban to reach the rocks himself, which in sunlight, would be no more advantageous than standing out in the open.

"Halliday …!"

Halliday recognized Masterson's voice but didn't respond.

"Listen to me. Doban was a thief and a madman. We called him a friend and were as helpful to him as we could be. But he betrayed us and he deserved to die. With you, it's a different proposition."

Halliday came to his feet and dusted himself down. Peering out from behind the boulder, he saw Rufe Masterson standing on the edge of the waterhole, a rifle across his chest, his shaggy beard hanging halfway down his chest. Jase and Aldo stood behind him, and in the moonlight, all three made as good a target as Halliday had ever seen. He leveled his gun.

"We want to be friendly, Halliday, and to show we ain't foolin', we're gonna hold our fire and let you have all the water you want."

"Why now and not before?" Halliday wanted to know.

"We needed you to lead us to Jake. We didn't want to keep huntin' him no more. You met him so you know what we're talkin' about. And now you've done what we wanted, we're in your debt. So come on down and nobody will try to stop you. When you've rested and slaked your thirst, all you've got to do is come to our camp and we'll talk some more."

Halliday watched as Rufe motioned to his son and Aldo, and all three disappeared up the slope. Halliday leaned against the side of the boulder and watched the moonlight gleam on the surface of the waterhole. He was so thirsty his tongue was beginning to swell. He wondered how Doban had lasted so long.

He waited five minutes, and when there was no sign of the three men, he slowly came out from behind cover. He walked carefully, gun in hand, his eyes sweeping the area beyond the waterhole, but no shots were fired. When he reached the pool, he dropped to his knees and drank, then immersed his head and shoulders beneath the surface. He kept his head in the water for almost a minute, and when he straightened — he saw Jase on one side of him and Aldo on the other. Jase pushed his rifle forward and said;

"Give us any more trouble and we'll blast you to hell!"

"Then you won't be able to use me," Halliday opined.

"If you keep buckin' us, we won't want to. It's got to be our way or none."

Halliday licked the water from his lips and knew he had made a fool of himself. Maybe it was this valley, because from the moment he'd ridden into it, he couldn't remember a single sane thing he'd done or said.

He got to his feet and Aldo turned and walked away with Jase trailing him. When they were halfway up the slope, Jase stopped and said;

"We've all been wastin' a lotta time and energy, Halliday, so now we're gonna bed down. Follow us and you'll find a place ready for you. Food, too. In the mornin', things will look different and we'll get along fine. You'll see."

Halliday wiped the water from his face and neck and watched them walk away. For the life of him, he could not believe any of this was actually happening, but then he turned and looked behind him and saw Doban's body in the moonlight.

After a second drink, Halliday climbed the slope and had no trouble following Jase and Aldo along a rugged ridge. He still had his gun and if Jase had spoken the truth, he'd soon have something to eat. Then if he played his cards right, he might get a good night's sleep and in the morning make some plans. And those plans would not include staying long in these parts. Most of all, he needed his sorrel and canteen.

It took only twenty minutes for Halliday to follow Jase and Aldo into a clearing surrounded by tall, healthy pines. At one end stood a solid, sizeable building with two doors and three windows in the ten-foot-high walls. At the other end were three smaller cabins with one door and window each. Between these was another flat-roofed building that appeared to be a barn or storeroom, and well away in an isolation of its own, was a weather-bleached tent. Jase and Aldo immediately headed for the biggest of the buildings without looking back at him.

Halliday stopped and took stock of his surroundings as soon as Aldo and Jase went inside. Lamps showed in all the windows, but there was no welcoming party, nor was there a hint of sound in the camp.

Keeping his gun in his hand, Halliday made his way toward the tent, pulled back the flap and found his blanket spread out on the floor with his saddle and saddlebags beside it. On a small box was a steaming plate of stew, four thick slices of bread and a tin mug with a coffeepot beside it.

Halliday turned and checked the clearing again, but it was still silent and empty. He went into the tent, sat on his saddle and after placing his gun within easy reach, ate hungrily. The food was tasty and the coffee was strong and hot.

Rolling a cigarette, Halliday sat and smoked and listened to the silence. He had no idea yet where the horses were kept, but he didn't think Rufe would be crazy enough to leave them too far from camp. Nor would he risk leaving them between the camp and the waterhole. So they had to be beyond the camp, and even with the aid of moonlight, his eyes were unable to pierce the blackness.

Getting to his feet, he tied back the flaps and stretched out on his blanket, using the saddle-bags for a pillow. In that position, he could see the building Aldo and Jase had entered and the three smaller cabins with lamps flickering in their windows.

Halliday rubbed a hand through his sweat-matted hair and figured the only thing that could improve his situation was a full bottle of whiskey. Knowing that was impossible, he pinched out his cigarette and flicked it into the clearing, then stretched out his legs, letting every muscle in his body relax.

Then, as if on some signal, all the lamps in the camp were extinguished and a feeling of utter weariness swept over him.

He had no trouble putting all thoughts of Jake Doban from his mind as he dropped off to sleep.

FIVE

THE MANHUNTERS

Buck Halliday had no idea how long he'd slept or what time it was when he was roused by the steady clip-clop of horses' hoofs from the far end of the clearing. He bellied his way to the front of the tent and peered across the clearing to see the distinct shapes of three horses and two riders disappearing down the trail he had used to get to this camp. Curious, he rose and bent to get his gun. But no sooner had he strapped the gunbelt on than a footfall outside his tent caused him to turn.

Rufe Masterson stood in the tent opening with his rifle in his hand, regarded him gravely and said;

"You must get more sleep, Halliday."

"Maybe I've had enough," Halliday replied. "And, just maybe, I need to get some fresh air into my lungs and see what that pair are up to."

Rufe smiled and shook his head. "You must not concern yourself about my son and Aldo Cobbitt. They are merely goin' to dispose of Jake Doban's body. And while they're away, I'll be watchin' camp, and I'll be so nervous about trespassers that I'll probably shoot to kill if I see so much as a moving shadow."

Halliday shrugged, then asked;

"How long do you think you can keep me here?"

"For as long as you are useful."

"Weeks? Months?"

"That depends on you, but I have the feelin' that you won't give us much trouble when you settle in. You strike me as a man who's drifted aimlessly, not knowin' exactly what you want from life. I think I can provide the answer. Now go back to sleep and don't leave the tent until one of my daughters summons you in the mornin'."

"I'm used to eating dust, roughing it and makin' my own decisions. You won't be able to change that."

"We'll see," Rufe smiled bleakly. "But perhaps the gambler in you will make you want to take a chance."

"Who said that I'm a gambler?"

"You gambled against Jase when you fought him and you gambled against Jake. On both occasions you won, which pleases me, 'cause I like a winner."

"Maybe I'll gamble on gettin' past you and findin' my sorrel," Halliday said.

"Then you'll lose," Rufe said, and untied the tent flaps and let them drop. He then walked away without another word.

Halliday stood there listening to his receding footsteps before he lifted the flap again and stood in the opening. Rufe was sitting on a tree stump, rifle across his lap, watching him from a distance of no more than fifty feet. His smile had not a trace of warmth in it.

Halliday let his stare swing past the big man to the area beyond the camp, but there still was nothing to be seen but darkness. He returned to his blanket, stretched out and closed his eyes again.

Sheriff Tad Toomey led his horse out of the yard to find seven men waiting at the mouth of the alley to join him. This small response to his request for a posse made him feel angry. But he suppressed the urge to berate the rest of the men standing around, and approached Ben Cullard.

"I'm leavin' you in charge while I'm away. See Lampert and Nathan are buried and do what you can to quieten Joel and his sister. And make sure Joel doesn't follow us."

When Cullard answered with a nod, the sheriff swung into the saddle, checked his posse again, then kneed his horse into a run. He knew he had a long and dangerous ride in front of him, and apart from worrying about what lay ahead when he caught up with Jud Drury and Cobb Blaney, he didn't like the thought of riding all the way across what was commonly called Hell's Trail.

It had been a year since he'd been called on to travel to Creede, and he still had vivid memories of the heat, the lack of water and shade, and the seemingly endless desolation which could make any man feel he had reached hell's doors. But he intended to succeed in this manhunt, even if it meant he had to travel beyond the border towns where his badge would be an open invitation to the local hellions.

Leaving Pardoo, he led the posse south, and although it was only an hour after sunup, the heat was so intense, he knew that by noon he and his companions would be burned to a crisp.

So, a mile out of town, he called a halt and brought the men together. His posse consisted of five young men of the hell-raising breed, two oldsters, Brad Browne, a self-confessed unambitious prospector, and Chance Larkin, a one-time riverboat gambler and now a saloon loafer whose stories of the 'good old days' became less credible with each new telling. To the men, he said gravely;

"We're huntin' two killers of the worst kind, so when we catch up with them, nobody has to play by any rules. When you see them, shoot to kill. I'll take all the responsibility after that."

"Ben said they was nothin' but backshootin', sneaky low lifers," Browne offered.

"An apt description," Toomey agreed. "But I reckon there's more of 'em and all of 'em's mean. They killed Nathan cold and that's what you've all got to keep in mind. There'll be nothin' to be gained by talkin' to 'em."

"What about Halliday?" Larkin asked. "Nathan came into the saloon before he visited you, Tad, and offered good money for somebody to ride with him. Nathan said Halliday raped his girl."

Toomey looked sternly at the man, and said;

"Forget Halliday. We're after Blaney and Drury."

Larkin exchanged a quick glance with Browne, who shifted his horse closer to the sheriff and said, gruffly;

"Nathan offered a hunnert dollars a man, and that ain't chicken feed."

Toomey became suddenly impatient with both of them. "Nathan's dead and can't pay you a dime, can he? But no matter. You joined this posse to run down Nathan's murderers — men who also robbed Ben after robbin' Jedro Plant up at Millicent. There's no money involved, apart from expenses, which will be paid by the town council when we get back."

Browne pursed his lips and again glanced at Larkin. "Guess we've been misled then, Tad. We figgered Joel or Lizzie would honor their father's offer when we brought Halliday in for hangin'. So if you figger on spendin' all your time huntin' down Drury and Blaney, Chance and me had better pull out now. Halliday's our priority."

Color flooded Toomey's face when he growled;

"You're puttin' money before your duty to the town and respect for a dead man?"

"Never did cotton to Nathan," Larkin said. "As for the town, guess everybody in Pardoo looks after hisself first. Always been like that, Tad, and nobody's ever gonna change it."

Toomey brought his fist down hard on the pommel of his saddle and snarled;

"Then get to hell outta my sight, both of you." He checked on the younger men. "Same goes for anybody else who isn't interested in huntin' Nathan's killers down."

85

The younger men shifted uneasily under Toomey's searching gaze, until one of them, who had only a month before started work at the saddlery, said;

"No need to bark at volunteers, Tad. Tom, Will and me were kinda taken with Halliday. We figured Dace was no loss to anybody, the way he threw his weight around. As for Lizzie, well, she always struck us as easy pickin's for anybody who took a shine to her. We're after Drury and Blaney, too."

Toomey looked slightly relieved and checked on the last two of the five — the Beetson brothers — Hal and Linus. Hal, the older of the two, muttered;

"Ben didn't deserve to be beat up and Nathan's bark was worse than his bite. We ain't so sure about Halliday, Linus and me, 'cept'n we ain't stupid enough to want to take him on. So count us in and let's get on with it."

Encouraged, Toomey again looked at Browne and Larkin. "Get in our way and we'll ride right over you. Got that?" Neither Larkin nor Browne appeared concerned with the threat, and turned their horses and rode away.

After watching them go, Toomey gathered the young men around and announced;

"Figger Blaney and Drury are headin' for Creede. Now, have you all got enough water and food for six or seven days?" The young posse men assured Toomey they had and the sheriff, sighing deeply as he tied his bandanna over his nose and mouth, led them into the searing heat of the desert.

In the three days they traveled across the desert after leaving Pardoo, Chance Larkin came to regard Brad Browne as something far different from the saloon time waster he'd previously thought him to be. The man had not only displayed skill in reading sign, but also the rare ability to cover a lot of distance without unduly exhausting his horse. Indeed, he'd been so successful that since sunup of the second day, there had been no sign of the sheriff and his posse behind them, despite the fact that the country was flat and barren.

Resting at a noon camp on the third day out from Pardoo, and with his enthusiasm for the journey already beginning to flag, Larkin managed to keep his irritability in check. After carefully measuring out a drink from his canteen, he stood in the shade of his horse, built a cigarette and said;

"You reckon we've come past the halfway point yet?"

Also standing in the shade of his horse, Browne screwed up his mouth and shrugged.

"No way of tellin'."

"But you've been this way before, haven't you?"

"Sure."

Waiting for more information, Larkin was annoyed when it didn't come.

"So, dammit, why *don't* you know? We been ridin' for three days and nights. Maybe you've got us lost."

"Ain't ever got myself lost, Chance, you can take that as gospel. But one thing I don't do when travelin' in country like this is take a guess at anythin'. Guessin' and bein' proved wrong takes the pepper outta a man."

Larkin took another drink from his canteen and Browne, after snorting in disapproval, said easily;

"Another thing I don't do is drain my water supply."

"Go to hell," Larkin growled.

Sweat ran down his face as he sleeved it away. He watched as Browne lifted his canteen to his lips for barely a second, then screwed the top on again and replaced it on the saddle horn. Then he climbed back into his saddle.

Larkin stifled a curse and glared defiantly.

"That all the rest we're gettin'? No more'n five minutes?" Browne was calmly studying the desert ahead. He scratched the stubble on his chin, then pulled his bandanna up to cover the lower half of his face and muttered;

"Come or stay, Chance. I'm goin' on till sundown, then maybe I'll rest up someplace for an hour or two before I hit the trail again. You see them hills ahead?"

Larkin saw towering blue shapes in the distance and said sourly;

"'Course I can see 'em. You think I'm blind?"

"Them hills are a trap. Knew a feller once on his way to Creede who strayed off the trail figgerin' that where there was hills, there had to be water. But all he found was heat that burned his skin black and dead trees and rocks. He said by the time he got back on the main trail, after losin' a day and a half, he was near dead and if he hadn't run into some folks on a wagon, he wouldn't have lived to tell the story."

"What story?"

"About them hills bein' a trap," Browne replied testily, and let his horse walk on. "So we ain't gonna head that way, but maybe Toomey and the posse will."

Larkin's interest was aroused.

"What about Halliday?"

"Halliday will know what gives. You can be sure he's no ordinary drifter, not the way he beat up Dace, got the jump on Toomey, violated Lizzie, then got clean away." He shook his head emphatically. "Nope, Halliday ain't gonna waste time ridin' hills he don't know. He's gonna be in Creede waitin' for us, and when we find him, all we got to do is kill him."

Larkin again found it necessary to wipe away the rivulets of sweat coursing down his face, and the fact that Browne seemed immune to the heat did nothing to improve his sour mood. But with the afternoon heat burning down and the wide, sandy desert before him, he decided to keep quiet and reserve his energy. But he promised himself he was going along with Browne for the last time. He'd let the man lead him to Halliday and then he could go to hell.

Thinking how he might help Browne along the trail to hell brought a thin smile to his cracked lips.

"Don't it ever end?" Luke Watson asked as he drew his horse alongside Tad Toomey's and checked on the drawn faces of the others in the posse.

"Everythin' has to eventually," the sheriff said, trying to console him. "We haven't passed any dead men yet, have we?"

"Meanin'?"

"Meanin' that Halliday's somewheres out in front of us, as are Drury and Blaney, with Browne and Larkin trailin' behind 'em. If they can make it, why can't we?"

"Drury and Blaney are desperadoes who know they're bein' hunted, that's why," Watson grumbled. "As for Halliday, I reckon he's built for this kinda thing, and Larkin's got Browne to show him the way. They say Brad once lived with Indians and ate buffalo meat and heaven knows what else."

Toomey inspected the faces of his posse and didn't much like what he saw. In towns, younger men almost always held their own, but out on the trail, where it often came down to a fight for survival, the old hands won out every time. He couldn't really understand why. He only knew that he had once joined a posse under Marshal Pontier, a man of fifty-five years of age, and after three weeks of dogging the trail of outlaws, Pontier had caught up with them and personally accounted for four of the six men — whereas Toomey and the three younger members of the posse had almost let the other two escape.

No, Toomey decided, if he had his way, he'd have preferred to be riding with Browne and Larkin. He said;

"Okay, boys, hear me out. It's gonna be just as tough goin' back as goin' on, so we'll keep ridin' with no more complaints. And keep your eyes peeled because pretty soon we're goin' to see somethin'. I can feel it in my bones."

The youths looked at him skeptically and Toomey knew he hadn't impressed them. He hadn't expected to. He knew their respect, even in town, was to the badge and not the man.

He rode ahead and listened to the creak of saddle leather and jangle of harness as they fell in behind him, and not once for the rest of the long afternoon did he stop, make conversation, or do anything but look stubbornly ahead into the shimmering heat haze which hung over the country like a heavy blanket.

SIX

OLD FRIENDS MEET

"Jake?"

The whispered name brought Buck Halliday's eyes snapping open, but he remained perfectly still. He had slept better than he had in months, although from time to time he had awoke with a thirst and helped himself to cold coffee. Now his eyes searched the darkness, aware that it had been a woman's voice that he'd heard, though he was unable to pinpoint her position.

"Jake, it's Mercy. Don't make a noise. Don't speak. I'll come in to you."

Halliday raised his head from the saddle and saw the tent flap lift and gray light filter past a shape kneeling on the ground. Then the shape wormed its way under the canvas and came slowly toward him.

"Pa's still outside, so be real careful. How do you feel after what they put you through?"

Halliday didn't reply. In the darkness, he figured he had some time before she became aware of her mistake. Then he heard her moving closer to him and a moment later, felt her hands sliding up his chest until they rested on his shoulders.

More than anything, Halliday wanted to find out what was going on in here, so he remained silent and even placed his hands on her back. When he felt her smooth, cool skin, a lot of memories came flooding back to him. Then Mercy's lips moved over his cheek, hungry for his mouth.

What the hell, Halliday told himself. Things like this happened in the most unlikely places and mostly when a man was least expecting it. His fingers on her back gently eased her against him. Then, just as suddenly as Mercy had shown her willingness to feel her lips on his, she pulled away, and Halliday heard her quick intake of breath.

"Your beard! What happened to it? What's going on?"

"You have the wrong man, Mercy," Halliday told her. "Sorry."

"You're not Jake!" Mercy cried, and pushed herself away from him.

Halliday held onto her wrists, hoping to keep her quiet. "No, Mercy, I'm not Jake Doban. But I'm a friend of his. I was on the other side of the valley with him."

Even in the poor light, Halliday could see her hands covering her breasts. Apart from that, he couldn't guess at her age or see her face, but he had a feeling that in a better light she would not be a disappointment. Those breasts had been firm and well-rounded, the rosebud nipples hard. He said;

"Let me explain. I was with Jake when he got killed. We were working together, trying to get out of this place. Jake wanted to find you and take you away."

"Dead!" Mercy breathed. "Jake's dead?"

"Aldo and Jase shot him. He didn't stand a chance. But while they were doing it, I reached the waterhole and I guess I was just too keen to drink to properly protect myself. They grabbed me and brought me here."

"This is Jake's tent," Mercy said sharply. "Why would they bring a stranger here?"

"Maybe with Jake dead, they figured I could replace him."

Mercy came slowly to her feet, and as the light improved, Halliday made out her tall and slender body. For a moment, he figured Rufe's plan to populate the camp might have some merit and maybe it wouldn't be such a hard way to pass the summer.

"Nobody can ever replace Jake," Mercy said after a silence. "He was going to take me away from here. We were going to take some pelts and gold and Jake said we'd be happy somewhere else. I know he was right. We were going to be married."

"So you don't like it here, Mercy?" Halliday asked, keeping his voice quiet in the hope that she wouldn't panic.

He'd already gained the impression that Jake Doban had spent a lot of time sweet-talking her.

"I like it," she said, surprising him, then knelt again, no more than an arm's length away. "It's just that I don't have a say about anything. Pa and Jase make all the decisions and my sisters go along with them. It's not right, is it, a woman not being able to decide for herself? Jake certainly said it wasn't."

"It sure isn't, Mercy," Halliday readily agreed. He sat up and reached for his shirt. "Tell you what. How about we go through with the scheme you and Jake had planned? You take me to the horses and I'll get you out of here. I'll see you settled someplace where you can do what you like, make your own decisions."

"Why would you do that for me? I don't even know you!"

Halliday was aware that already she seemed to have forgotten all about Jake Doban. Maybe she wasn't bright, or maybe Rufe's rigid lifestyle had slowed her thinking. Either way, he figured he had a chance to talk her into helping him.

"You'll get to know me, Mercy. Jake and I hit it off well and if he trusted me, you can, too."

The light was getting better by the minute, and her face was taking shape. She was young, smooth-skinned and decidedly pretty. But the fact that the light was also bringing her naked body into clearer perspective began to disturb him.

"I don't know what to think," she said. "I relied on Jake and he let me down. My sisters have been angry with me over our relationship, and pa hardly lets me out of his sight."

Remembering Rufe and his threats, Halliday's nerve ends tingled. Within a half-hour it would be daylight and all chance of escaping today would be gone.

He got to his feet, buttoned his shirt, pulled on his boots, then strapped on his gunbelt. Mercy made for the side of the tent, indicating that she was ready to leave.

"The horses," Halliday reminded her. "Where are they?"

"Just past the big house."

"Anyone else up yet?"

"I didn't see anyone."

Halliday checked his gun, then he rolled up his blanket and shouldered his saddle. Moving across to her, he said quietly;

"Why don't you get something to wear and wait for me with the horses?"

Mercy looked at him curiously.

"We'll go away?"

"Why not?"

"What about the pelts and the gold? Jake said —"

"Forget what Jake said. I've got plenty of money, land, everythin' we'll need, in fact."

When she smiled at him, Halliday had the uncomfortable feeling that traveling with Mercy was going to present some problems. She lifted the side of the tent and light filtered inside. For the first time, he was treated to a full picture of her, and had to stop himself from reaching out to her again. Then the flap was pulled back and more light filled the tent.

Heeling around, Halliday stared straight down the barrel of Rufe Masterson's rifle, and the fiery look in the man's eyes left no doubt in Halliday's mind that he'd need very little provocation to pull the trigger.

Seeing her father, Mercy cried out, shot under the tent flap and disappeared.

Halliday dropped his saddle and spread his hands in a gesture of submission.

"Jake made the same mistake, Halliday," Rufe said. "I thought you were smarter'n him."

"A man's got to try something," Halliday protested.

Rufe sadly shook his head. "You don't understand. Mercy's my youngest. She doesn't realize what I'm tryin' to do for her. But the others do, and they'll kill you if you try anythin' like this again. Breakfast is ready at the house."

"We're all goin' to sit down and talk. That it?"

"And the sooner the better. My other girls will watch over Mercy from now on, so you won't be alone with her again." He lowered the rifle and wiped his face with his sleeve. His eyes looked suddenly sad. "Can't you give it a try? My time's short and before I go, I want to make sure I've left somethin' behind. Can't you understand that?"

"I think you're crazy," Halliday told him. "It won't work. Even if your daughters give you grandchildren, the little ones won't grow up overnight."

Masterson shook his head. "I'll start with three and next year there'll be another three. Then I'll bring a woman in for Jase and in hardly any time at all my family will grow." He waved his arms expansively. "In four or five years, there'll be people everywhere. The air's clean, the soil's rich, and nobody will find us."

"Jake Doban did, and so did I," Halliday reminded him.

"Mistakes that won't happen again. The boys have buried Jake and you're goin' no place. So why don't we all get friendly?"

Halliday breathed a heavy sigh. He had been in some strange situations, but none as strange as this.

"So let's eat and talk. Who knows, there might be somethin' in it for me."

"I'm sure there will be," Rufe assured him, and held out his hand. "Just a precaution."

Halliday hesitated, but only until Rufe leveled his old rifle on him and his eyes gleamed threateningly. He drew his gun and threw it to the old man. Rufe slid the gun into his belt and backed out of the tent. When Halliday joined him outside, he saw Jase and Aldo waiting in the clearing, and behind them, two young women standing in the doorways of two of the three isolated cabins. But there was no sign of Mercy.

"Pork and eggs, washed down with our home-made rotgut. Then we'll take you on a tour and let you decide for yourself."

Halliday eyed the old man carefully.

"What if I still say I want out?"

"We'll kill you and look again," Rufe said, and waved Jase and Aldo toward the main building.

When they went from sight, Rufe led the way across the clearing and as he followed him, Halliday looked at the women. They had identical shaped bodies but their expressions and provocative stances, with the early sunlight penetrating their flimsy dresses and displaying their rounded hips, convinced him that they were going to be more trouble than Mercy.

He followed Rufe inside and found Mercy, dressed now in a loose-fitting frock, serving breakfast at a long table which extended halfway down the room. Against a wall were two crude bunks with a third at the other end. Apart from the table and the stools which lined each side, the only other items of furniture in the building were a huge iron stove and a table standing beside it on which were stacked pots, plates and eating utensils.

Rufe pointed to his place at the table, waited for Halliday to sit down, then gestured for Aldo and Jase to seat themselves. Mercy didn't acknowledge Halliday's presence, nor did she stop serving breakfast when her sisters began to make up the bunks. Then Rufe steepled his fingers, lowered his head and intoned;

"We give thanks this glorious day for ..."

Halliday gritted his teeth. Glorious day? Like hell ...!

SEVEN

TRAIL JUNCTION

At sunup on the same morning that Buck Halliday ate breakfast with the Mastersons, Chance Larkin and Brad Browne reined their horses down beside a section of newly-turned ground.

Having ridden through the hottest night in living memory, Larkin was in such a sour mood that not even the discovery of a grave could take his mind off his own misfortune.

"So somebody died and somebody buried him. So what?"

"Fresh dug," was Browne's quiet response. "Guess we should check it out."

Larkin scowled blackly at him. "Check what out? You ain't gonna dig up no body while I'm around."

"Might be Halliday," Browne reasoned. "If it is, we're wastin' our time trailin' him, ain't we?"

Larkin wiped sweat from his jaw line. Only an hour earlier, he had been forced to beg water from Browne, and although he had let Larkin moisten his lips, Browne had made it clear that he wouldn't give him anymore. So Larkin had decided that very soon he might have to take action.

"You do the diggin'. I ain't touchin' no body."

"Superstitious?"

"Nope. Hot."

Browne swung out of the saddle and ground hitched his horse. He found a branch, broke it under his boot, and using the jagged end, began to dig.

Larkin sat his horse, glaring down at him, his hand on his gun and his mind in turmoil from thirst and mounting hatred.

"Lousy towners," Cobb Blaney said from the cover of a huge boulder where they'd been hiding since they first sighted the men leading a horse with a dead body slung across its back.

Weary from their long ride and short on provisions and water, the pair had watched the grave being dug and the dead man buried. But neither of them had been disposed to confront the men, firstly because they didn't give a damn who killed whom or who buried what. Second, because at no time did the two men expose themselves to open attack.

In the end, Blaney had decided to risk an attack, but before he could execute it, the two riders had gone back across the desert toward the mountains. In the darkness of night, Blaney had decided to take no risks, but stay where he was and rest up during the cool hours.

Now these two had arrived in the early morning and he recognized them as having been in the saloon when they'd robbed the saloonkeeper.

"Reckon they're huntin' us?" Jud Drury asked, watching as one of the men dug his way down into the grave and feeling his shoulder.

"What in hell else?"

"They mentioned Halliday," Drury reminded him, wincing.

"What's it matter? They got water and mebbe food in those saddlebags. You want to die out here?"

Drury certainly did not want to die, here or anywhere else. He just wanted his shoulder wound tended. So he drew his gun.

"I'll get the digger, you get the other one," Blaney said.

Drury nodded, and a moment later, the morning's silence was shattered by the roar of guns.

105

Blaney's bullet hit Browne squarely in the back of the head and the prospector pitched forward onto his face. Drury's shot was equally as lethal. It hit Larkin in the side of the head, knocked him from his horse and left him lying on the ground.

Blaney and Drury waited until the echoes of the gunshots had faded, then waited another five minutes to see if the pair were alone. When no one else rode into sight, they approached the gravesite. Blaney toed Browne onto his back, grunted, then went to Browne's ground hitched horse. After searching the saddlebags, he removed the canteen from the saddle horn and helped himself to a mouthful.

Drury caught Larkin's horse and sourly announced;

"This jasper didn't have nothin' in his saddlebags. Dammit, why do I always come up empty-handed?"

Blaney drank again before he tossed the canteen across to Drury, and while the little man drank, he bent and searched through their pockets. He found a tobacco pouch, a pack of playing cards and eleven dollars in bills and change. After dividing the money, keeping the cards and giving Drury the makings, he went back and collected their own horses. Still counting the money, Drury said;

"What now?"

"We head for the hills."

Drury looked across the heat-shimmering distance and growled. "Why not ride to Creede? We can get lost there or recognized. We ain't known 'round those parts."

Blaney shook his head and swung onto his horse, then muttered, "You don't see everythin' you should, do you, Jud?"

"Like what?"

"Like the look of those mountain men. You figger they've been starvin' lately or dyin' of thirst?"

Drury screwed up his mouth. He had been impressed by the size of the riders and the effortless way they'd dug the grave in the hard ground.

"So?" Drury asked, still confused.

"So they've been eatin' and drinkin'. And we got somethin' on them, too, haven't we?"

Drury's frown deepened. With a sigh Blaney explained; "We seen 'em bury a dead man. That ain't lawful, is it?"

"So?"

"So we'll tell 'em to help us or we'll turn 'em in."

"Who to?"

Blaney smiled bleakly. "Well, maybe we won't tell 'em who. We'll just lay it on the line and make a deal. I heard them mountains were a death

107

trap, but it seems that's a lie, like most other things I've heard about these parts. You comin'?"

Drury swung tiredly into the saddle, looked along the trail to Creede, then shrugged.

"Hope you're right. I'm about sick of this heat."

"Better times ahead," Blaney told him, and led the way across the desert toward the hills.

It was noon when Sheriff Tad Toomey threw up his arm and motioned for his posse men to rein in. Through eyes reddened by glare, he studied the scene before him. He saw a bearded man lying beside a newly-turned grave and his companion nearby, lying on his back, sightless eyes turned to the sky.

Larkin and Browne …?

Behind Toomey, Luke Watson said in a shocked voice;

"By all that's holy, look at 'em!"

The others stayed back, faces drained of color.

"Wait here, Luke," Toomey said. "Keep the others away until I've checked things out."

"They're dead," Watson replied. "So we ain't likely to disturb anyone."

"I want to check the ground for sign that might give us a clue to what happened."

Watson accepted the explanation and watched Toomey ride on. But after waiting a short time, his curiosity got the better of him. He swung out of the saddle, told the others to stay put, and approached the dead men.

When Toomey saw Watson approach, he smothered his anger at the young man disobeying his order and pointed out the marks in the softer ground leading to a cluster of boulders.

"Two men on foot."

"Killed them from cover?"

"Looks that way. Stay here, Luke, while I look around."

Watson followed Toomey behind the cluster of boulders, where they soon agreed that two men had rested there for several hours and had left their horses in cover further back in the rocks. When they returned to the others, Toomey announced;

"Seems Larkin and Browne came upon a grave and wanted to know who was in it. Before they could dig it up, two men shot 'em from those rocks back yonder. I don't know why exactly, but it's my guess the killers were Drury and Blaney."

Watson eyed Toomey with interest, and asked;

"How come you figured that?"

"Drury and Blaney are killers. And they would know that they'd be hunted. Making a comparison of the time it took us to get here, and the time they set out ahead of us, I'd say they'd have been able to rest up here for hours. And the killers did wait around in that nest of rocks for some time."

"That's smart, Sheriff. But why would they kill Larkin and Browne and not just let 'em go? They weren't wearin' badges and weren't part of any posse, were they? Also, they weren't huntin' Drury and Blaney but were after Halliday."

"Drury and Blaney wouldn't know what Browne and Larkin had on their minds," Toomey countered. "So when they saw them arrive and start to dig up the body in that grave, they musta figgered they were dangerous. Also, seein' as Browne and Larkin no longer have anythin' in their pockets, they were robbed. Bein' on the run, they wouldn't let a chance to rob somebody slip through their fingers."

Once again, Watson was impressed.

Aware that he'd at last impressed Watson, whom he considered to be the mouthpiece for the others, Toomey walked back to the grave and dragged Browne's body away. He then picked up the branch Browne had used, knelt and began to dig earth from the hollow. Watson suddenly let out a yell;

"What the hell are you doin'? That ain't right, diggin' up somebody already laid to rest."

"I've got to see who it is. You don't have to watch. In fact, none of you boys have to watch. Pull back till I'm finished."

"Like hell we will," Watson growled. "You'll bring down a curse on your head which might affect the rest of us. And ain't we got enough bad luck already with all this heat and dust?"

Toomey looked up solemnly. "I'm runnin' this, Luke. If you don't like what I do, pull out like Browne and Larkin. Could be you'll meet the same fate."

Watson's face tightened and he looked quickly at the others to gauge their reaction. When he found them pulling back, he smothered a curse but added;

"Who do you expect to find in there?"

"Mebbe Halliday. Who else? As far as we know, apart from ourselves, the only persons still traveling this trail are Drury, Blaney and Halliday. Mebbe Drury and Blaney sighted Halliday, shot him and buried him. If they did, and unearthing the body will prove it one way or the other, they'll be charged with another murder along with the rest of their crimes."

Watson had no more argument to voice. He withdrew to watch Toomey dig the earth away. When he suddenly let out a curse, Watson quickly stepped forward again and stared down at the battered, blood-and-dust covered face of a man he had never seen before.

It wasn't Halliday, and despite feeling nauseous, he was relieved.

"Looks like he went under a stampede," he muttered.

Toomey nodded and began to kick the dirt over the body again. This time Watson helped, and within minutes, they'd covered the body and stamped the ground back in place. Only then did Toomey remove his bandanna and wipe his face.

"Jake Doban," he said, and the pronouncement of the name with such certainty brought a frown to Luke Watson's young face.

"You knew him, Sheriff?"

"I was asked by the Red River lawmen to keep an eye out for him and notify them if he ever came into my bailiwick. They'd hunted him for weeks but lost him near Millicent. He was wanted for murder and robbery. He's better dead and I'll be glad to let the authorities know. Now, we'd best bury the others."

This time Watson quickly organized a burial party, leaving Tad Toomey to scout ahead. By the time Browne and Larkin were laid to rest, Toomey had returned with the dead men's horses, which he handed over to Hal and Linus Beetson, then pointed straight out across the desert toward the mountains.

"If it is Drury and Blaney we're on to, they went that way. The tracks are clear enough."

The posse men looked in dismay at the heat-choked country before them, but it was left to Watson to again challenge Toomey's plans.

"Aren't they the dead mountains, Sheriff, that everybody says to stay away from?"

"That's them," Toomey confirmed. "And that's where our killers are headed. I'm gonna run 'em down."

"They say there's no water out there," Watson complained again. "And the way I see it, we're gettin' mighty short already. How far away is Creede?"

"Another two days," Toomey told him. "But if you check the trail, you won't find any sign of travelers. We go west from here." Toomey let his horse walk into the hot sand of the desert and didn't look back. He had ridden a good fifty yards when he heard the first sound of movement behind him, then the Beetson brothers ranged up alongside. Watson followed, with his two companions in tow. The sheriff looked at each man in turn before he said;

"I've got to go on but the rest of you are not bound to follow. Whatever you decide won't be held against you if you pull out. Maybe you're just not up to it."

The young men said nothing, and when Toomey rode on and they fell in behind him, he felt a warm feeling inside him.

For the first time since he'd pinned on the badge in Pardoo, he knew the satisfaction that acceptance of a responsibility gave. Tying his soiled bandanna around his nose and mouth, he put his horse into a walk and even the hot sun seemed to have lost some of its intensity.

He was certain Drury and Blaney were ahead of him and nothing mattered more to him than to run them down and take them back to hang.

In the company of Aldo Cobbitt and Jase, Rufe Masterson took Buck Halliday on a tour of his camp. Although Halliday was impressed with the fertility of the valley beyond the camp, and felt obliged to congratulate Rufe on his plans for the future establishment of a town, his main interest was in discovering the place where Rufe kept the horses. But at no time did he even hear one.

Returning to the main building, Rufe had Aldo and Jase move the long table, then lift a trapdoor in the floor to reveal a ladder leading to an underground cellar. Descending first, Rufe asked Halliday to follow him.

When Halliday joined him, he found himself in a storeroom crammed with pelts, two walls lined with barrels and crates and a third with crude but solid shelves holding an assortment of firearms, gunpowder kegs and a hundred or so canvas bags.

Crossing to the shelves, Rufe took down one of the bags, removed the tie-string and poured gold nuggets into a gnarled and grimy hand. His eyes gleamed when he held his palm in front of Halliday's face.

"Enough to buy me a town just as soon as the women do their bit. What do you think?"

"Where did it come from?" Halliday asked.

"Straight outta the valley. You seen the wash down the northern slope, didn't you?"

Halliday nodded.

"Up top there's a crevice where the wash begins. We don't even have to dig for it, just wait until the water washes the nuggets and some specks down. We been collectin' it now for close on a year, and that's what we got."

He pointed to two shelves sagging under the weight of more gold bags.

"Every now and again, Jase and Aldo head off to Creede and buy provisions. They pay for 'em with gold."

"Risky, isn't it?" Halliday said.

Rufe grinned widely. "Nothin' risky when Aldo and Jase are involved. Hell, I figgered you'd already know that. They do their buyin' then just head out. If anybody was to follow 'em, they just lie in wait and kill 'em, then double back in their own good time. What we got in mind is to buy reg'lar and disappear so's not to excite any interest in us. Come another year, we'll have everythin' we need to start the town. The valley's got plenty of lumber and there's water aplenty, and the ground's so fertile it'll grow anythin'. Given five good years and we'll have farms and lumber mills, and mebbe even a saloon."

Halliday's eyes widened. "You figure a saloon goes with your church?"

"Why not? A man can't pray all day. Anyway, when I'm established as the head of the family, I don't expect ev'rybody to become teetotal. I'm an easy man to get along with, as you'll see." Halliday smiled but Rufe didn't seem to care.

"Wealth and comfort like you never had in your life. And my girls as well."

Rufe looked Halliday over keenly and nodded several times. "First time I seen you ridin' in, I liked the cut of your rig. When you tricked Jase and showed you could take punishment as well as dish it out, I knew we'd found somebody who belonged. You're better than Jake Doban, the miserable, double-crossin', schemin', thievin' scum. So what's holdin' you back?"

"Murder," Halliday said calmly.

Rufe couldn't hide his surprise.

"You call gettin' rid of Jake murder?"

"He was shot down after being almost driven mad by you huntin' him. And what did he do, apart from wantin' to marry one of your daughters and not all three?"

Rufe gaped and backed away as if Halliday had struck him. "What did he do? Why, he bucked my law, Halliday, tried to turn Mercy agin me, then tried to rob me. That was the thanks I got after I'd taken him into my home and offered him a life he couldn't get anywhere else at any price." He shook his head emphatically and glared at Halliday. "Not murder ... justice."

"What about the men you said Jase and Aldo laid in wait for and killed when they trailed them?"

"Thieves, scum, spies out to take what we have and spoil what we got planned. That's not murder, that's plannin'."

"And if I try to leave?"

Rufe eyed him fiercely and his colorless lips tightened. "You'd be a fool to try and I know you're not that. You give me a month of your time and marry my girls meantime — all three of 'em. When they tell me they're with child, you can have all the gold you want, provisions, your sorrel and a clear trail outta here. How about it?"

"I wouldn't get a hundred yards out of the valley, and you know it," Halliday told him.

"You have my word," Rufe growled.

"The word of a murderer and founder of a cult. You're crazy and your schemes will never come to fruition. Why not just pack up, take your family and Cobbitt someplace else and let them settle down and make their own lives?"

Rufe shook his head. "You still don't understand, do you? I don't want strangers in my family. The bloodlines have got to be pure. I'll be the head and the only rules will be mine. I'll spend my last years watchin' 'em grow. Everybody here will be a Masterson."

"Except Aldo Cobbitt," Halliday reminded him. "Is he wise to what might happen to him?"

A trace of concern showed in Rufe's eyes for a moment, but quickly died.

"Aldo believes in me," he said quietly.

"More fool him," Halliday said.

He turned and stared up the narrow stairway that led to the floor above. Aldo was looking down on them, frowning heavily. Halliday gave him a shrug, but almost immediately Jase eased Aldo aside.

Rufe pushed Halliday roughly toward the stairs. When the drifter had climbed up, he followed and kicked the trapdoor closed, then waited for Jase and Aldo to move the long table back in place.

"I ain't gettin' anywhere with this jasper," Rufe told Jase. "So mebbe you'd better take over for awhile. But I don't want him beat up as much as Jake was because I got the feelin' that he ain't all that tough. It won't take much to change his mind."

Jase lifted his hands to his belt and rubbed his knuckles on the buckle. When he flexed his massive shoulders, Halliday felt a chill run down his spine.

Halliday then looked at Aldo and said;

"This is maybe your last chance to get out, Aldo. If you don't take it, these jaspers are goin' to use you, then kill you."

Aldo's face darkened and he glanced across at Jase, who said;

"He's lyin', Aldo. We need you and like you. Pa will look after all of us and pretty soon ev'rythin' will be fine."

"Get on with it," Rufe bellowed.

As if released by a spring, Jase stepped forward, his huge arms lifting and his fists clenching. Halliday stepped back but Rufe jabbed the barrel of his rifle into his back and said gruffly;

"If he tries to run, stop him. Then you can spend some time with Glory and Charity and I'll see they behave 'emselves."

An eager look came into Aldo's eyes, but he smiled uncertainly. Halliday knew then what control Rufe had over the man.

Halliday stepped forward and feinted with a left. Jase didn't bother to dodge it but closed in, huge arms swinging.

One fist cracked against the side of Halliday's head. The drifter's feet went from under him and he hit the floor. Through a haze, he saw the blurred shape of Jase's arms reaching down for him. He tried to move out of range, but Rufe's rifle pushed him back. Then Jase's hands gripped him and Halliday found himself lifted from the floor as if he were an empty sack.

With superhuman strength, Jase swung Halliday above his head and held him there. Halliday tried to get a hold of Jase's shoulder but the big man only lifted him higher. Halliday struggled in the iron-fisted grip, but Jase merely tightened his hold until Halliday felt as if his bones would break.

Then a shout came from outside, followed by the sound of running footsteps. Halliday could see nothing but the rafters above his head, but felt Jase's grip slacken.

"You ain't allowed to come in here, Charity," Rufe bellowed.

The footsteps stopped and then a young woman's voice was clearly heard in the room.

"There's two riders comin' up from the waterhole."

Halliday felt himself being lowered but Jase's grip still held him firm.

"You sure?"

"Seen them plain, pa. One's a big man and the other's small and dirty."

There was a moment's silence before Rufe cursed bitterly. Then his gravelly voice said;

"Put him down, Jase. I'll watch him. Charity, how close are they?"

"Two hundred yards away but coming on slow, like they ain't sure where they are."

"They'll soon know where they are, by hell. Hurry now and get your sisters in position. You know what to do. Jase, you and Aldo get ready."

Halliday found himself shoved roughly against the wall with Rufe's barrel digging into his jaw. He glanced sideways, saw the young woman in the doorway and was momentarily stunned by her beauty. Her golden hair framed a face so perfectly-featured she looked as if she had stepped out of one of Halliday's most cherished dreams.

Long-limbed and with the sun behind her, she exuded health and untouched youth. The too-small blouse which only half-covered her full, rounded breasts and the bandanna-sized black skirt around her hips suggested she had dressed in a hurry.

When she went from sight, Aldo and Jase followed her at a run.

Left alone with Rufe, Halliday had no opportunity to be grateful for Charity's timely intrusion because Rufe forced him across the room to stand at a rear window. From there, with the gun again pressed to his jaw, Halliday saw Charity tear her clothes from her body. By the time she reached the three cabins, Mercy and Glory had come into their doorways. Charity shouted anxiously and they quickly disappeared indoors to come out a moment later, both naked. Then, linking arms, they paraded up the clearing. There was no sign of Aldo or Jase, and as yet, no sign of the trespassing riders.

"Make one sound, Halliday, and you're a dead man," Rufe said. "Just watch."

Having no other choice, Halliday let his gaze follow the women up the clearing.

EIGHT

ONE OR THE OTHER

Sight of the naked women left Jud Drury flabbergasted.

"Cobb, do you see what I see or am I sufferin' from heatstroke?"

Cobb Blaney rode to the top of the rise where Mercy, Charity and Glory had stopped within a hundred yards of them. Their naked bodies were bathed in sunlight, and each swayed back and forth, their hair swishing across their creamy shoulders and their chanting reaching the ears of the dumbfounded riders.

"What in all hell?" Blaney exclaimed.

Even though Blaney couldn't take his eyes off the captivating sight, he drew his gun, while

Drury looked around and found the rest of the clearing deserted.

"I want me some of that, Cobb," Drury said excitedly. "If I'm dreamin', I'll shoot you through the heart if you try to wake me."

"Don't forget the two men," Blaney warned. "Their tracks led right to this place."

For a moment, Drury's eyes became solemn, but a louder chant from the women brought his attention back to them. Wiping his mouth on his sleeve, he touched his horse lightly with the toe of his boot, ignoring Blaney's dire warning.

Seeing him ride toward them, the sisters began to separate, waving and urging him on. Drury's eyes lit up and his body became tense. Blaney called again, but Drury was beyond listening. He slowed his mount as he drew rein beside Charity, completely captivated by the enticing smile and the young face.

Never in his eventful life had anything like this happened to him.

When the young woman made no attempt to run away, all thoughts of danger vanished from Blaney's mind.

"You sure are somethin' to see, girl," Drury said. "Please tell me I ain't dreamin'?"

Charity's smile was warm and welcoming as she stood before him, her body swaying from side to side. When she failed to speak, Drury slipped from the saddle, hitched up his gunbelt, and wiped his grimy hands on his shirtfront. He was within a few paces of her, his hands beginning to reach out for her, when the explosion of a single rifle shot shattered the silence.

Jud Drury stopped as though he had hit a wall. The impact of the bullet spun him around so that he could see Blaney, gun in hand, trying to quieten his horse. Blaney's face was filled with fear as Drury called out, weakly;

"Cobb! What in—?"

Then his legs buckled and blood trickled down his face. He fell on his side and rolled onto his stomach, fingers clawing at the dust. Blaney looked on in horror as Drury convulsed and lay still, his face buried in the dust.

Ignoring the threat of Blaney's gun, the women came together again and stood staring at him. But Blaney was now only interested in survival. His eyes swept the timber that lined the clearing but he saw no sign of a rifleman. Then a voice called;

"Drop your gun or you get the same as your friend."

The voice came from Blaney's right, but when he looked in that direction, all he saw were rocks and timber. The sun beat down on him and an eerie stillness settled over the clearing. Then the voice called again;

"We'll get you before you c'n move ten feet, mister. So do as I say."

Blaney drew rein as sweat stung his eyes. He couldn't believe any of this — naked women, Drury being shot down and him threatened with death if he made a false move. Yet he felt he had some chance of escaping if he turned his horse and sent it hard into a gallop. Before he could do anything, Charity said;

"If my brother says he'll kill you, he will, mister."

Blaney's stare swung back on her. He was shocked by her indifference to her nakedness and the dead body that lay at her feet.

"Your brother?"

"We'll treat you well if you give us no trouble," Charity told him. "We might have need of you."

Blaney blinked against the glare, then stared down at Drury's unmoving body.

"N-need me?"

A chill went down his spine when he didn't recognize his own voice. Then Charity pointed to her sisters.

"All three of us. Pa will give you a test and per-haps he might prefer you to the other man."

Blaney wiped his face but began to perspire again, still seeing no sign of the gunman.

"Your pa?"

He tried stalling for time, hoping that an opportunity to escape might present itself. If it did, he'd sure as hell take it in both hands.

"This is pa's place and we are his family. We have everything here that's needed for our future. Won't you put your gun away and let us show it to you?"

When Blaney jerked his gun a little higher, Charity's mood suddenly changed.

"If you don't, you will certainly die. So put up your gun."

Blaney licked his lips and turned in the saddle, eyes searching the timber again. Then Jase Masterson and Aldo Cobbitt appeared, both carrying rifles. Blaney cursed under his breath.

"We don't want to kill you, mister," Aldo called out. "We might have need of you."

"You killed my friend," Blaney said scathingly.

"We had no need of him," came the quiet reply.

Blaney wiped sweat from his eyes and studied the three women. The only part of all this that seemed grounded in reality was that his friend was dead. Then he remembered how sudden it had been. One shot, dead center in the forehead.

He tossed his gun to the ground and even as it bounced, Charity, Mercy and Glory turned and walked away, their bodies gleaming in the sunlight.

"Wait a goddamn minute!" Blaney yelled.

But the women kept walking. When they each entered one of the cabins, Blaney turned in the saddle. He jumped when he saw that the two riflemen were already within a few yards of him.

"Get down," Aldo ordered.

Blaney obeyed without protest. Jase picked up his gun and pushed it into his belt. When Aldo put a hand on Blaney's shoulder, Blaney shrugged it off. But Aldo put it back again, more firmly this time. Staring fearfully into Aldo's cold eyes, Blaney felt his shoulder buckle under the powerful grip.

"Okay, okay," he yelled. "Ease up. I'm not buckin' you."

"Then walk to the house," Jase said, and pointed to the building at the far end of the clearing.

Aldo walked to Blaney's horse and led it away as Blaney stepped around Drury's body and gulped air into his lungs. This whole thing was impossible to believe. The sun must have addled his brain.

Then he looked back and Drury's body was still lying there. He gulped hard and decided to play it for what it was worth. At least they hadn't killed him. Then he thought of the woman who had spoken to him.

Hell, he had never seen a body like that before …

"That's about the gist of it," Rufe said. "You've ten minutes to think it over, then I want your answer. But I warn you, I'll not tolerate deception or lies, and if you break your word, you'll die."

Having heard the old man out, Cobb Blaney stared stupidly across at Buck Halliday. When they'd brought him to the house, he'd wanted to kill Halliday. But now, knowing firsthand the strange things that went on here, yet still not fully believing them, his hate for Halliday was pushed well into the background. He looked at Halliday and said;

"Is this for real?"

"It's for real," Halliday replied.

They'd both been given a glass of sour mash and Halliday's stomach still churned. On top of that, his thoughts were a little jumbled, proving that not only were the men and women here way out of the ordinary, but the liquor was something else again. "I don't believe it," Blaney protested. "Jake was here?"

"*Was*, is right," Halliday told him.

Blaney wiped sweat from his upper lip, looked gravely at Rufe and asked;

"Why me?"

"You happened by," Rufe told him.

Blaney sat back, the sour mash doing its job. He grinned and pointed at Halliday.

"We didn't just happen by, Rufe. We came lookin' for that jasper to shoot him."

"You might still get your chance," Rufe said. "Only one of you will win here. The loser, naturally, cannot be allowed to leave to talk about our family and our plans."

Blaney leered at Halliday. "Give me one chance at you, Halliday, and so help me, I'll kill you."

"You might get that chance," Halliday said.

He'd watched from the window when Aldo led the horses away. He'd gone straight to the end of the clearing and it was five minutes before he returned. So, Halliday figured, given the chance, he could get to the horses in well under a minute — if he knew exactly where they were.

"Give our visitor another drink, Jase," Rufe said. "Then we'll leave him here to think over our proposition. Meantime, Halliday, you do some thinking, too."

Halliday sat back and folded his arms. He realized that for all his grandiose plans, Rufe made plenty of mistakes. One was having Jake Doban buried along the trail to Creede, and allowing Aldo and Jase to leave tracks.

How else had Blaney and Drury found this hellhole?

Also, he depended a lot on the loyalty of the women, and Halliday had always considered women were more likely to look after themselves before others — even kin. So, just maybe, Rufe would make another mistake.

Aldo left the building while Jase and Rufe remained in the doorway. After studying Rufe for some time, Blaney asked; "I get the women? That's what you're tellin' me?"

"And you'll be looked after better than you've ever been in your life, and when you have fulfilled your part of the deal, you'll be paid in gold and allowed to leave."

Blaney took Rufe at his word, then looked at Halliday. "Why wouldn't you do it? Didn't the women get to you?"

"Just thinkin' about them now stirs my blood," Halliday grinned easily. "But I've got a healthy regard for my hide."

"Scared of them?" Blaney challenged.

Halliday shook his head and nodded in Rufe's direction. "No, but I'm scared of him, his crazy son and his mixed-up hired hand. When Rufe gets what he wants, and has no more use of you, he'll kill you."

"Then mebbe I'll stay. Why would I want to leave, with what's them gals are offerin' me?"

"The choice won't be yours," Halliday said.

Blaney looked quickly in Rufe's direction and Rufe came slowly across the room to stand at the head of the table.

"You have my word that in due course you will be allowed to leave. Now, I think you've had enough time to think about it, so give me your answer."

Blaney pushed his thumbs behind his belt buckle.

"Mr. Masterson, you just signed on a new hand."

Rufe beamed and called for Jase and Aldo.

"You heard?" Rufe asked them.

Both men nodded.

"Then it only remains to get rid of Halliday. I think our new friend should be the one to do that, don't you?"

"Is he capable?" Jase asked.

"We'll see," Rufe said, and looked at Blaney again. "You professed a deep hatred for Halliday. Am I correct?"

"You never been more right."

"Then we're gonna let you kill him. From what you've said, I've gathered that you're good with a gun."

"Few come better," Blaney boasted, but shot a wary look in Halliday's direction.

"And more than capable with your fists?"

"I can hold my own."

Rufe seemed delighted again. He walked back into the doorway and looked out into the sunlight. Then his face lifted toward the sky and his lips moved in silent prayer. Just for a moment, Blaney had misgivings, then Aldo took him outside and Jase brought Halliday out. Rufe pointed to the edge of the clearing and announced;

"It will happen there. Blaney, I want you to prove to all of us just how good you are. It will help you with the women, too, because what they want, and what I want, is a capable man like my son and like Aldo could have been."

Aldo escorted Blaney to the side of the clearing and Jase motioned Halliday to follow them. Then Rufe called to the women, and when they arrived, dressed and wide-eyed with excitement, Rufe announced;

"The fight will be to the death. When you've killed the intruder, you'll become one of us and a glorious life will be yours."

When Blaney eyed Halliday curiously, Halliday said quietly;

"They'll tear you apart whenever they want. But together, we stand a chance."

"Getting nervous?" Blaney taunted, and Halliday shrugged and dropped his hands to his sides.

Rufe nodded at Blaney and the big man lumbered in, hands held high. Jase and Aldo stood back, resting on their rifles as Blaney circled for a moment, then charged.

Halliday went under his first wild swing but held his own punch back. Snorting angrily, Blaney charged again … but with the same result.

Halliday then danced out of his reach, until Blaney taunted him again by yelling;

"Stand still and I'll knock your head off your shoulders!"

"You're just not up to it!" Halliday told him.

Roused to uncontrollable rage, Blaney charged again, but this time Halliday stood his ground.

Snapping out a straight left, he jolted Blaney's head back and brought him to a sudden halt. Hurt, Blaney swore fiercely, and threw himself at Halliday. But Halliday let him come, ducked and brought his head up hard under the big man's chin. Stunned, Blaney sagged forward and Halliday dipped his shoulder under him and heaved, sending him flying over his back. When Blaney fell, the left side of his face hit the ground and his eyebrow split open. Blood spurted.

Halliday watched Blaney struggle to his knees, then told Rufe;

"He's nothin' but a fool."

Anger flared in Rufe's eyes and he stepped up to the dazed Blaney and kicked him hard in the stomach. When Blaney fell again, Jase lifted him off the ground with one hand and planted him on his two feet. Aldo was grinning and the young women were looking only at Halliday.

Blaney swayed, but Jase held him upright, then turned to his father.

"He's nothin' like Doban or Halliday, and Doban's dead and buried. Mebbe you gotta think again, pa."

"I've done my thinking and made my decision!" Rufe roared. "I can't trust Halliday. I could never trust him. But this weaklin' will suit our plans just fine. Get their guns."

Blood dripped down Blaney's face as his stare settled first on Jase, then Aldo and finally on the crazy-eyed Rufe.

"He got the jump on me. But I know I can take him."

"He'll eat you up!" Rufe snarled. "And we don't want you so bad hurt my girls won't wanna look at you. Clean yourself up."

Rufe turned to his daughters, and after a moment's thoughtful study of their faces, he asked;

"Will Halliday suit you?"

Charity looked first at Blaney, then at Halliday. The corners of her mouth curled derisively when she again turned her gaze on Blaney. Then she said coldly;

"What must happen, must happen quickly. Already there's been too much delay. We'll take the winner and be done with it, but then the boys must keep a better lookout. How is it Jake found us, then Halliday and now two others? What's gone wrong?"

"Plenty's gone wrong!" Rufe shot back. "But nothin's goin' wrong again, I swear."

"I hope not," Charity said, and her tone brought a deep frown to Rufe's brow.

"Meanin'?"

Charity drew herself to her full height.

"Meaning that we want it over and done. We belong to you and we're proud to be able to start a family. We'll bring up our sons in your image, but it must be soon."

"Or?"

Charity pointed to Glory and Mercy. "Glory will become more restless and Mercy more uncontrollable. You've promised us so much but so far you've given us nothing."

"And you?"

"I'm your daughter," Charity said quietly. "But I'm also a woman."

136

Rufe's hands lifted and his face flushed.

"Are your desires turning your head, girl?"

There was little anger in his voice now.

Charity shook her head, the sunlight gleaming on her hair.

"You encouraged us to think of the future, and we want it fulfilled. It's that simple. There's to be no more parading, no more delays. Give us our man and the rest will follow."

Rufe pursed his lips and swore under his breath. Then he again looked to the sky as if seeking inspiration. Aldo was studying Charity hard, but there was nothing but disdain for him in her eyes. Then she looked at Halliday and a thin smile broke out on her lips.

Rufe saw the smile, scowled, then ordered Jase to get the guns. By then, Blaney had cleaned the blood from his face and was glaring at Halliday.

"I'll kill you now."

Jase returned, handed Halliday and Blaney their guns and escorted Blaney twenty paces up the clearing. He then lifted his rifle, leveled it and said;

"No tricks. Aldo will see Halliday pulls none, either. When pa gives the signal, draw and fire until one of you is dead. Understand?"

Blaney licked his lips and gave an uncertain nod. Then Rufe moved to a point halfway between Blaney and Halliday and nodded.

Blaney's hand shot down toward his gun. His draw was swift and smooth and the weapon cleared leather in a blur of movement. Halliday had been watching Blaney's eyes and had seen nothing but hatred. He had no great desire to kill anyone, but he didn't want to be killed, either.

As Blaney's gun came up, Halliday's right hand dipped and his gun cleared leather. Blaney's body jolted to one side at the last moment, but Halliday remained calm and relaxed. The explosion of one shot broke the day's silence. None of the onlookers moved.

Then Blaney stumbled back a pace, then another and suddenly the gun fell from his fingers. His knees buckled and he went down as a growing patch of red appeared in the center of his shirt. He lifted his hands to the wound and without a sound, fell forward on his face.

Rufe exchanged glances with Aldo and Jase before he stared hard at Halliday.

"None of my men are that fast, Halliday. You're welcome to join the family now. But I warn you, I want no more trouble. If necessary, I'll have you bound."

Jase moved forward and took the gun from Halliday's hand. Under the threat of rifles, Halliday had no option but to relinquish the weapon. He stared down at the unmoving Blaney. He'd had no time for the man, but he hadn't wanted to kill him. These crazies had made him do it, and although he had killed before, this killing left a bad taste in his mouth. He said;

"I won't obey any of your fool rules. You can believe it."

Rufe scowled and Jase glared. Then Aldo stepped up to Halliday and brought his gun barrel down on the side of Halliday's head. As Halliday fell unconscious, Rufe grunted his approval and turned to his daughters.

"You'll be ready for him when he comes to and we've cleaned him up. How you manage it is your business, but whether it takes a week or a month, I don't want to see any of you until it's done. Hear?"

When the daughters nodded and walked away, Aldo effortlessly lifted Halliday from the ground and slung him over his shoulder. Following Rufe and Jase, he headed for the door.

NINE

BLOOD ON THE MOON

It was late afternoon when Sheriff Tad Toomey led his posse down the narrow trail to the waterhole. Despite the fact that they were short of water and the surface of the waterhole looked invitingly cool, the sheriff held his men back.

"Be careful," he warned. "They could have seen us comin'. We've come this far so don't make a mess of it now."

The young ones bunched up behind him, each man eyeing the waterhole. After so much heat and dust, they all wanted to throw themselves into the pool. Yet during the long ride, they'd come to respect Toomey as a lot more than a symbol of authority. He hadn't made a single mistake.

"Doesn't seem to be anybody about," Luke Watson said. "Guess they got the water they wanted and rode on."

"We'll see," Toomey said, coming out of the saddle and handing his reins to Watson.

In a crouch, he made his way down the slope, gun in hand. Even when he reached the waterhole, he squatted in deep shade and let his eyes sweep over the surrounding terrain. The blanket of heat that fell over him was suffocating and brought sweat to his face, neck and hands. He wiped his hands dry on his shirtfront and took a firmer grip on his gun butt. The silence filled him with an uneasiness that he'd never known before.

He stayed there for five minutes before he rose and stepped out of the shade, expecting at any minute to be dodging bullets. But he reached the edge of the waterhole without being challenged, knelt and carefully scooped a handful of water into his mouth. He swallowed the water after swilling it around his mouth, and he sighed as its coolness trickled down his throat. Turning, he beckoned to the others, and when they rode noisily down the slope, he had to restrain himself from yelling at them.

It had been a hard ride for him, but harder for them.

The youths drank, watered their horses, then filled their canteens. It was a brighter-eyed group who sat their saddles later while Toomey took stock of their surroundings.

As far as he could see, the country beyond the waterhole was nothing but a barren wilderness. He turned his attention to the near side of the waterhole and saw hoof prints leading up through the brush. Leading his horse, he made his way to the top of the slope and came out onto a plateau. Here, his vision was hampered by thick brush, and beyond it a forest of timber.

Waiting for the others to reach him, Toomey scouted around and found tracks of more than two horses. On closer inspection, the trail seemed to have been used by a lot of people of late. Pointing this out to his men, he said;

"Don't know what's ahead of us, but those fellers came this way. What they're up to or where they are, we'll soon know. So we'll leave the horses here. Just keep your eyes peeled."

There was not a word of argument, and after tethering their mounts in the shade, the posse moved out on foot.

Toomey found the rest of the trail hard to follow as it led first one way then another, at times circling back on itself. The heat was unbearable and when he finally stepped out into a clearing and a cool wind hit him in the face, he felt like yelling with excitement.

Instead, he dropped onto his stomach and stared across a dusty clearing at three cabins, a tent, and at the far end, a large building.

The others dropped to the ground, and complete silence settled on them, until Watson said;

"I heard there was nothin' up here but rocks and critters. So what's this?"

"The walls of those buildings are unweathered, so I reckon they've been built recently. What the hell the tent's about, I haven't any idea. You see the smoke?"

Watson nodded. A thick spiral of smoke was coming from the chimney of the big building.

Toomey inched forward until his head and shoulders protruded beyond the brush. But just as he was coming to his feet, a tall man carrying an old rifle came across the clearing, heading in their direction.

Toomey ducked back behind cover, hoping he hadn't been seen. But the man stopped suddenly, brought the rifle up to his shoulder and stood glaring his way. When Toomey swore, Luke Watson said;

"I ain't ever seen him before. Sure ain't Drury or Blaney."

Toomey pushed Watson back as the rifleman started to walk toward them. He remained in hiding until Aldo Cobbitt was no more than fifty yards away, then showed himself by stepping from the brush and letting the afternoon sunlight gleam on his badge. He held his gun down by his side, his nerve ends were tingling, his breathing ragged. Sweat glistened on his brow.

Aldo stopped in mid-stride, holding his old rifle across his chest. Neither man spoke, before Watson stepped out of the brush, and one by one, the others followed him.

Toomey saw Aldo's stare sweep over the men but nothing showed in the man's face to indicate what he might do.

"We're lookin' for two men who rode in here. I'm Sheriff Tad Toomey from Pardoo, and my intention is to take those men back to town to stand trial."

Aldo showed little reaction, except to slowly lower his gun then turn so that it was leveled on the sheriff.

Toomey felt his skin crawl, mostly because the vacant look in Aldo's eyes suggested he didn't understand. Then Watson said;

"We ain't lookin' for trouble, mister. Mebbe you can help us. We'd sure be obliged."

Aldo's finger moved onto the trigger and his eyes narrowed. Behind Toomey, Hal Beetson said hoarsely;

"Watch him. He looks a mean cuss."

"The rest of you stay behind cover," Toomey told them. When he took a step forward, Aldo's rifle bucked in his hand. At the last moment, seeing the finger whiten on the trigger, Toomey threw himself sideways and shouted a warning to the others. Watson threw himself the other way and Aldo's shot whistled past his shoulder. Even as he hit the ground and began to wriggle back into the brush, Watson heard a high-pitched scream from behind him.

A twig ripped a gash in the side of his neck but he ignored the pain as he kicked furiously to make more room for himself. Finally flattening enough brush so that he could move freely, he lifted his gun but before he could fire, another man charged right over him.

Watson was forced to hold his fire as Linus Beetson burst out into the open to be hit full in the chest by a savage burst of rifle fire. Seeing Linus go down, Watson tried to scramble to his feet, but another heavy body came toppling down on top of him and he threw up his hands just in time to fend Hal Beetson off.

Wild shooting erupted all around them as Watson struggled to get away from Hal's body. He saw Toomey smashing his way deeper into the brush and swore, thinking he was trying to escape. But even as he was preparing to shout abuse, the sheriff took cover behind a deadfall and the other two posse men raced across to join him.

Aldo was still standing in the open, blood running from a cheek and a gash in his forehead and shattered bone protruded from a third wound high on his left shoulder. His eyes were vacant and Watson couldn't believe that he was almost begging to be killed.

Bullets were still smashing into Aldo as Watson looked down at Hal, seeing him lying on his back, sightless eyes turned to the sky. Then he checked on Linus and saw him flat on his face in the sunlight with half his face blown away.

A tremendous fury surged through him and he kicked savagely at the flattened brush as he cleared a passage back into the clearing.

Aldo's expressionless eyes turned toward him, and for just a moment, Watson thought he saw a glint of satisfaction. Then the big man pumped off two more shots, one of which took the still advancing Watson in the chest and the other tearing into his shoulder. He stumbled sideways, his gun discharging into the ground as a thunder of guns continued on his left. Even as Watson fell, he saw the big man stumble backward, straighten himself, then slowly begin to buckle. His rifle fell from his hands and he collapsed on top of it, but Watson saw no more from that moment as pain surged through his body and darkness claimed him.

Knowing they had finally killed the tall rifleman, Toomey told the others to hold their fire. He checked the clearing but there was no sign of anybody, and after the rattle of heavy gunfire, the silence was nerve-wracking. He called out;

"Luke, you all right?"

There was desperation in his voice because he believed he already knew the answer. Standing beside him, the two young men were white-faced and silent.

"Luke?" Toomey called again, then stepped past the men and made his way toward the unmoving body.

When he turned the body over and saw the gaping wounds, he cursed viciously. He stepped away from Watson and checked on Hal and Linus Beetson. Both brothers were dead.

Toomey stood shaking his head, tears forming in his eyes and his body beginning to tremble.

Three young men who had offered to help him were dead, savagely butchered by some loco fool!

Toomey rubbed his hands over his face as if hoping to erase everything. Then he looked out into the clearing at the killer. Even from this distance, he could see a dozen wounds in the rifleman's body, and kept asking himself;

"Why?"

Then the two youngsters were beside him, and one, who was the same age as Luke Watson, took one look at Watson's body and staggered away. Toomey swore when he heard the man retch. Then the other young man said;

"Why'd this happen? We weren't gonna hurt that crazy loon, were we, Sheriff?"

Toomey shook his head.

"He started it and near finished it. You hurt, Sheriff?"

"No. You?"

The man shook his head dismally.

"Never got a scratch, yet Linus, Hal and Luke are all dead. They ain't ever done nobody any harm. I mean, apart from kicking up their heels from time to time."

"They were good men," Toomey allowed. "The best."

The other man returned looking as pale as flour.

Toomey then quietly made his way back to the fringe of the brush and checked the clearing again. Seeing three young women running hard from the cabins toward the big building, he stopped dead in his tracks and went to ground. When the young men joined him, they were in time to see the women disappearing through a side door past a man equally as big as the one they had just killed. Then Rufe Masterson came to the doorway and shook his fist in the air. The three young men exchanged worried looks before one said;

"What in all tarnation is this? This place ain't ever been spoke of, has it, Sheriff?"

"Not that I know," Toomey said.

The door of the building was slammed shut and deep silence settled around them. Toomey looked at the sky and wiped sweat from his brow.

"Three women, two big men and one old codger. It don't figure."

"It sure enough is real though," the second youngster said. "You figure the man we killed was protectin' these women?"

"From what?" Toomey asked angrily. "I had my gun down by my side and he had his rifle. He must have known I meant him no harm. And I told him I was a lawman."

"Maybe they're outlaws," the first man put in. "We ain't sighted Drury or Blaney yet, have

149

we? Maybe they rode here on purpose, knowin' they'd be welcome. Then when you showed yourself and your badge, that crazy loon started blastin'."

Toomey thought about it for a long time before he shook his head.

"No, if Drury and Blaney are with them, wouldn't they have joined the gunfight? There's somethin' mighty strange goin' on here, and I'm gonna find out what it is. I'm also gonna see that the deaths of three good men are avenged."

Tom Secombe and Will Wyatt exchanged worried looks, before Wyatt said;

"We gonna fight the women, too, Sheriff?"

Toomey swore again.

"We'll wait till dark, then get close enough for me to talk to 'em. I'll try explainin' and demand an explanation in return. Dependin' on what comes of it, we'll take whatever action's necessary. You still with me?"

Secombe looked back at Watson's body and sucked in a breath.

"Luke an' me was savin' up to start a freight business. We had it figured that in another two years, we'd be old enough and have enough money to run a line through to Creede. Now Tom ain't gonna drive no freight and I got no stomach for doin' it on my own. I guess I don't care much whether I get out of this alive or not, but somebody's gonna pay for what happened."

Toomey laid a consoling hand on his shoulder and looked at Wyatt.

"I ain't ever made no plans for the future, but I wouldn't have minded cowpunchin' with Hal and Linus in a year or so. Mebbe they wouldn't have wanted me along, but I sure enough would've gone had they asked."

"They won't ask now," Secombe told him.

Wyatt's lips tightened and he looked angrily up the clearing. "No, I guess they won't. But, Tad, you don't have to ask me if I'm stayin' or not."

Toomey settled down on his haunches and did some more hard thinking, and finally came up with a plan.

"Come sundown, we'll work our way as far as we can toward the big buildin', keepin' behind cover all the way. No matter what else happens, I'm not pullin' out till we clean this mess up."

TEN

PLANS GONE TO HELL

Buck Halliday studied the twitching face of old Rufe closely. He sensed that the oldster was beginning to lose hope.

"That man out there is Sheriff Tad Toomey from Pardoo. Aldo killed some of his men."

"And they killed Aldo," Masterson shot back angrily.

"Aldo started it," Halliday countered. "We all saw that."

The women were sitting across the room, and since they had entered, had not looked at Halliday nor spoken to him. "They were trespassin'!" Rufe defended.

"They couldn't know that," Halliday replied. "There's no warning signs, even if you do have legal right, which I doubt."

"The land's mine," Rufe stated. "I'm gonna build a church and have my daughters start my flock. I ain't havin' no trespassers gettin' in the way."

"Want them or not, Rufe, you've got them. Toomey is the kind of man who gets things done."

Rufe's eyes brightened and he shook his fist. "He won't get out of here, Halliday. He and his friends will all die. I swear it."

Halliday glanced at the women, found each of them staring at the floor, Charity and Glory expressionless, Mercy looking troubled. He said;

"Toomey is shrewd, Rufe. He won't take risks again, and won't trust his luck. Come sundown, I reckon he'll give you hell."

Rufe looked keenly at Jase for a moment and finding his son grave-faced, he said;

"What if he does? Don't you think we're up to takin' care of a bunch of no-account badge-toters?"

"Aldo wasn't," Halliday told him.

"Aldo don't matter. He did fine out there."

Rufe crossed the room and took Jase aside, and for several moments, talked earnestly with him. When he returned to Halliday, his mood had brightened.

"Now you'll see just how strong we are. We'll corner those scum and put paid to them. Then we'll get on with the business of you and my daughters."

Halliday shrugged and said, "You can't make me cooperate. Don't you know that?"

"They'll see you do, make no mistake. They're the finest-looking women ever born to a man. But if you still persist in buckin' me, I'll whup you till you beg for mercy. A week, a month, it don't matter. My destiny is assured."

Jase opened the door and went out into the dying light. After watching from a window, Rufe returned to usher the women to the trapdoor in the floor. Lifting it, he pointed down and said; "I want you to wait down there."

Charity and Glory went without protest, but Mercy held back, casting a quick, worried look at Halliday.

Rufe quickly laid a hand on his youngest daughter's shoulder and said, "It's gonna be all right. Everythin' is gonna be fine. Jake was no good and neither were those others."

Mercy licked her lips and Halliday could see that she was fighting to make a decision. But then Rufe eased her down the stairs, shouting for Charity to light the lanterns. When light filtered up from below, he closed the door. Turning, he found Halliday trying to get to his feet. Rufe rushed across the room, reversed his rifle, and swung the stock at Halliday's head. Halliday ducked and the stock hit the wall and splintered.

Swinging the rifle back, Rufe again missed, but then Halliday brought his tied feet up, catching Rufe in the groin.

Rufe dropped to the floor and Halliday swung his feet and caught him on the side of the jaw. Rufe whimpered, rose to his knees, then collapsed.

Halliday heaved himself to his feet and worked his way across to the table. Turning his back, he worked the rope against the edge of the table, sawing furiously until the rope parted. With a deep sigh, Halliday pulled the remnants of the rope from his wrists and untied his ankles. He was rubbing circulation back into his hands when Rufe began to stir.

Halliday raced across to him but he was still several paces away when Rufe dived to one side and grabbed his broken rifle. Halliday lunged and Rufe lifted the rifle by its shattered stock and fired. Halliday felt the burn of the bullet pass his head as he ducked his head to the side.

He reached for the old man but Rufe showed surprising agility as he ran toward the trapdoor. Before Halliday could reach him, Rufe lifted the trap as a thunderous outburst of gunfire shattered the sundown silence outside. Rufe leveled his rifle and snarled;

"Don't come any closer. I won't miss next time."

Rufe ran across the room, and from the window, saw his son staggering under a barrage of bullets. He cried out in anguish when Jase went down. With insane anger burning from his sunken eyes, Rufe walked toward the trapdoor, ignoring the bullets now hammering into the walls of the house.

Then a bullet shattered the window and creased his forehead. He went down on one knee as Charity's face appeared from below.

"Stay put. I'll take care of this."

Another bullet smashed into Rufe's back and he jerked under the impact, blood splattering Charity's face. Even then, carrying two wounds, Rufe managed to push Charity down the stairs, then began descending after her. When only his head was visible, he rested his rifle on the floor and took aim.

Halliday realized he had to make a run for it, and headed for the door. The shooting from outside had stopped and he was halfway across the room before Rufe fired a second shot, then a third. Halliday felt the whip of the bullets past his head and drove himself harder. He had the door open when he heard a cry of frustration and glanced back to see Rufe disappearing down the stairs.

He dived out into the clearing as Toomey and two young men came out from cover. Toomey's gun came up with a jerk but Halliday yelled out his name, then moved quickly to one side, in case Toomey and his companions panicked.

"What in thunderation is going on here?" Toomey called.

Halliday waited no longer. He broke into a run, joined Toomey and the others and pushing them roughly, yelled;

"Take cover."

"To hell with cover," Toomey shouted back. "We've come this far."

"There's only a demented old man and three of his daughters to fight you now. Wait it out, for hell's sake."

The urgency in Halliday's voice made Toomey obey him. They took cover behind a deadfall and stared silently at the big house for a long time, before Toomey asked;

"What's this all about? And how in hell did you get mixed up in it?"

"It's a long story," Halliday told him.

There was a deafening explosion and the roof and walls of the house were blasted skyward. The ground shook and the trees trembled.

"Holy Hannah!" Wyatt said, awestruck, and then another explosion drowned any comment the others might have made. This was followed by a third, and a fourth explosion and the clearing was blown up from one end to the other, until finally, the whole rocky slope above the waterhole fell away in a landslide.

Rubble, brush and rocks flew everywhere and all the four could do was flatten themselves and wait for the inevitable.

It seemed an eternity before Halliday deemed it safe to raise his head. His back felt as if somebody had pounded it with a hammer, but when he rose to his knees and then to his feet, he found everything intact. Looking down on the others, and seeing them still cowering behind the deadfall, he said;

"It's over."

Toomey looked up, a smear of blood showing on one cheek, but otherwise he seemed unscathed. Despite a swelling on his jaw, Wyatt looked okay, too. As did Secombe.

"I don't know how … but we made it."

Halliday walked away from the deadfall and took stock of the destruction. Where the big house had been, there was nothing but a deep hole. He remembered that during his inspection of the underground cellar, Rufe had shown him boxes of dynamite beside the stacks of pelts and bags of gold.

He knew then that the old man had made plans for this day of destruction in case things went wrong. The shame of it all was that he had taken his daughters with him.

Halliday looked across the clearing. There was one place old Rufe hadn't taken him on his tour of inspection.

Calling for the others to follow him, he led the way and found a thin ribbon of track leading down to a rocky hollow. Standing in the quiet were five horses. Saddles had been stacked under canvas and hay had been strewn around. They saddled the horses, and Halliday led the way down to the desert.

They rode until they reached the trail to Creede. Under the wash of moonlight, Halliday looked in that direction. Sensing he wanted to leave, Toomey snapped;

"You can't just leave us like this! We want to know what the hell this was all about."

"There's a lot I don't know myself," Halliday admitted.

"So tell us what you do know."

Halliday tried to make it all sound plausible, but it was not an easy thing to do.

Toomey looked incredulous. "His three daughters?"

"Beautiful, too," Halliday said.

159

"Which reminds me," the lawman began, "Nathan came into my office accusing you of rape."

"You know that isn't true, Sheriff. You know Lizzie, just as these others do."

Wyatt smiled crookedly, and said, "I sure hope that one day Lizzie takes a shine to me. She sure is somethin', isn't she?"

"Yeah, isn't she?" Secombe added.

Halliday shrugged. The sooner memories of Pardoo faded, the better he'd like it. But for the young men's benefit, he said; "She sure is that."

"So what do I do about the charge?" Toomey asked.

"I'm the one who should be layin' charges, but in the interest of peace and quiet, I'm just gonna forget it ever happened. My advice would be for you to do the same. It's been a pretty successful week for you otherwise, Sheriff. See you."

Toomey opened his mouth to argue, but Halliday was already on his way. They watched until he had gone from sight, then Wyatt said;

"Mighty strange feller, that. Bet he's got a story to tell." The lawman pushed his hat to the back of his head and smiled. "And my guess is that you're too young to hear it."